Chronicles
Of
Rhodran

A. R. BROWN

This book is a work of fiction. Names, characters, places, and incidents are the products of the author's imagination or are used fictitiously. Any resemblance to actual events, locales, or persons, living or dead, is coincidental.

<u>DEDICATION</u>

To my mother, who has always supported me first

and best in everything that I do, no matter what.

CONTENTS

<u>ACKNOWLEDGMENTS</u>

Firstly, I would like to acknowledge my mother, who was always the first to encourage me to follow whatever dreams I had to try to make them come true;

Next, my brother, father, and the rest of my family, for being there for me;

Last but certainly not least, my teachers, especially the high school ones that brought literature to life for me, taught me why it was so important, and inspired me to a love of reading and writing.

My library wouldn't be nearly as full without any of you.

PRONUNCIATION GUIDE

Rhodran - "Ro-dran"

Teldros - "Tell-dross"

Machdur - "Mac-dur"

Paledat - "Pal-e-dat"

Jasmer - "Jazz-meer"

Asvartha - "As-var-tha"

Laubadar - "Law-bad-ar"

Valwardus - "Val-ward-us"

Rorzkar - "Roars-car"

Horzkar – "Hoars-car"

Eordwar - "Oard-war"

Rordgur - "Roared-gur"

Targarma - "Tag-arm-a"

Regartha - "Ray-gar-tha"

Arkdhar - "Arc-dar"

Erzadhar - "Ersa-dar"

Varthulus - "Var-thoo-lus"

Cordaru – "Kor-daar-oo"

Avarthu – "Ahh-var-thoo"

Karvarthuk – "Car-var-thook"

Urdharmus - "Ood-harm-us"

<u>INTRODUCTION</u>

When I finally decided to take the leap and set out to write my first book, I knew then and there that it would have to be about dragons. Like many others, I have a lifelong love of the lore and mythology behind these enigmatic beasts. No one knows exactly where in the depths of the human mind these creatures come from, but undoubtedly they are here to stay. In some form, they are known to so many cultures, which attests to their enduring and unforgettable nature.

However, my perception of dragons has always

been different when compared to the norm. I don't see them as simple obstacles to the protagonist; simply brutes with no mind of their own. I rather see them as intelligent, sentient, and very much capable of a level of civilization which marks such beings. In my imaginings of them, I perceive them as capable of speech, just like humans, and this would, to my mind, be the reason for the animosity between the two species. We humans are okay with animals, because it is easy to see the differences and not feel threatened when there is no power of thought and speech, but give those faculties to a creature that adds to them strength beyond what humans possess, and it is easy to perceive it as a grave threat to our supremacy.

That puts humans and dragons on the level of two alpha predators in the same environment. The resultant clashes would be simply inevitable. That's why I set my story in an alternate future where, after a catastrophe that wiped out humans and most of the other species, the dragons stepped in to fill the vacant spot, and became earth's top alpha predator, like dinosaurs and humans before them.

This lack of any predators to check them would certainly allow this evolution, and once they reached that level, I envision that they would use what remained of human society to bolster theirs. That's why I depict them as using, with modifications, many of the same things that we do. However, due to their own choosing, they do not pick up a lot of the more sophisticated technology that we would leave behind. The raw materials, such as metal, stone and wood, I see as being reused to their purposes.

Dragon magic, meanwhile, would also expand. Here, too, I differ from some, and have more than just fire for a dragon's use. The evolution that the species went through allowed them to adapt to new environments and to claim use of the elemental forces of that environment. I see a dragon type's elemental abilities as not only allowing them to control and create their element, but to exist in it: fire dragons can survive lava and flames, ice dragons are adapted to the cold and snow, and so on.

As for their social structure, I see them as a very tight hierarchy. They have a much more robust treaty system with each other, and value each individual's contribution to society above all else. They are in this way, even more social creatures than humans.

While the aforementioned social structure and strong alliances prevent most conflicts, war does happen. When it does, though, it is, like the rest of their society, mostly carried out with the level of technology

4

that would be associated with medieval human societies. This is due to the dragons unanimously agreeing to leave the humans' most powerful and destructive weapons advancements buried in the rubble they left behind.

The structure of the realms is also hierarchical. The high king of all five realms is always the current king of the realm of Rhodran, and then in precedence behind him follow the kings of the other four realms as they joined the alliance; the ice realm, the fire realm, the water realm, and the earth realm. The realms all depend greatly upon each other, not just for economic, but military support. Should any one realm get aggressive towards another, or an outside force threaten, the others will ally to put an end to it. During times of dire emergency, if possible, they will convene a great army with soldiers from all the realms, and the high king at the head.

Being myself a great fan of reading and writing, I couldn't neglect to add among the characters a mage, scholar, and mentions of scribes. My personal view of dragons includes them being intelligent enough to be studious, and adapting, along with other things, the art of writing and language from humans. Their writings would be in a dragon script, created by them specifically for that purpose.

As far as physically, the dragons in my story are once again different from the standard depictions. Evolution has allowed them to stand on two legs, and their front legs have been adapted into arms for holding and carrying, complete with opposable thumbs that fully evolved from their dew claw digit. They still have wings, and tails; and like humans, like to adorn themselves and use garments, however, they have really only adapted breastplate armor and cloaks out of all the possible choices, as these are the least obstructive to the use of wings for flight.

Dragon's flight ability has changed, as well. The current form allows for further flight than before, and more agile, too. Their bones have lightened as well as their frames, and this allows for fairly long distances covered. However, in practice, when going somewhere outside of one's realm, other modes of transport are often favored rather than flying.

This is the world that my characters inhabit when a long defeated threat rears its head again. The individual character's response is what will end up shaping the future of this world. While each of them have a different motivation, it becomes clear that all of them are equally important to the effort.

Asvartha, the princess of Rhodran, seemingly has little in the way of combat skills, but in the end plays an important part in the final defeat of the threat. She as well as the others in her group have hidden skills that, as is often the case, only come out when needed the most.

Rordgur, the scholar, also would seemingly have little to add to the combat skills of the group,   and yet manages to prove his worth, both in his area of talent and in other ways.

All the main characters are protagonists that are surprising in some ways, while typical in others. Almost all of them use both their brains and brawn, rather than just strength alone, and the final battle is not just the group of five dragons using brute strength to win out over another strong opponent. I have always liked stories in which the hero or heroes show cleverness and strength, whatever forms those two might take. It takes both of them to win, and I like to show that.

Nor is the final battle won alone. Many stories have one hero going alone against the antagonist, and the others in the hero's group, if any, are not involved. I wanted to include all of them, as I felt it was their due, they worked just as hard to get to that final battle as the protagonist, and deserve to take part in it.

This in turn allows what happens next, which is one thing that fits the standard: the heroes, through their battle, go back home with better skills than when they started.

The mage improves her magic, the princess her leadership skills, and so on. They each had something to gain from the experience.

One of the things that I liked most about the

process was that it was a chance for me to not only create, but inhabit a world while I was writing.

I greatly enjoyed the time I spent inhabiting their world while writing this story, and I hope you will, too. Enjoy your stay in the dragon realms!

PROLOGUE

Earth had once been a planet that had boasted almost innumerable species, but since the great cataclysm there had existed only a few. The unaccountable thing was that, having protected themselves by hiding away, one of these species was one long thought to be either extinct or nonexistent by the dominant species they replaced; these new dominant creatures were the dragons. These scaly reptilians had restructured everything after ascending as the dominant species in the aftermath, and now had settlements all over the place. It had been many thousands of years since then, and the healing process had long been complete, as well as the changes that dragons had made to the landscape.

The lands, which were sparsely occupied now, had long ago been divided up into the various realms, each one with a king and royal family. The dragons had lived in peace for many generations, with only one short interruption, which was caused by the selfish desires of an ambitious adviser who thought himself to be a better choice to rule than the king. Aside from that one instance, which was long ago relegated to the abyss of memories, all the lands had long been rebuilt and the scars had long disappeared. Even the oldest individuals of all of the elder dragons were not yet hatched when that great conflict had occurred, and many of the younger ones, as many do when something is so far outside of personal experience, almost dismissed it as simple fairy tales, barely even looking at it as history.

In one of the realms that the dragons had divided up, this one called Rhodran, the lives of its citizens had long been steady and smooth. They did the same thing day after day, and never complained, because the rhythm and repetition of it all comforted them.

In this realm of Rhodran, every dragon had a part to play, and did it well. One such dragon was a young landholder's son, of a family who lived in the provinces, not far from the capital, who had been sent out today to cut some wood in the forest. Some would be for them to stockpile, for the colder weather was soon to come; the rest would be sent to town to be sold in the market so they could buy other goods they needed.

That would, in fact, be his likely job tomorrow, and

he would be expected to not only take the load to the market, but also to obtain as good of a price as he could, either through barter or money. One time he remembered he had even gotten a bunch of produce in exchange for some wood, from an earth kingdom merchant. They would have plenty to eat for the winter if he could do that again, or perhaps an animal for meat, to cook and salt and store away. He always liked going to the market, but the only thing he regretted was the sore muscles he'd have after carting those loads back and forth.

Thinking of very little but the job to be done, and the food and warm winter's cloak it would buy him and his family, the young green dragon continued on, with only occasional checks to make sure there were no dangers around. Few predators were left nowadays, and none that could really pose a big threat to an almost fully grown dragon.

All in all, for a dragon, he was about average: about seven and a half feet tall, although he wasn't quite full grown and would get a little taller, with powerful wings, and strong muscles. He was a green dragon, so he had dark green scales, and his belly scales were of a lighter green. He stood on his hind two feet as legs, and held the ax in his left front paw, which served as a hand. He swung the ax forcefully as he chopped; as a reptile, he was quite proportionally muscular.

The young dragon had left his large wooden wheelbarrow nearby, in which he was loading his wood to be able to haul it home. After a few trips, he began hearing some noises. He looked, but couldn't see anything nearby. He decided to return to his work, as it didn't sound as if whatever it was could be anywhere nearby, and he needed to hurry, as the afternoon was wearing on. Soon it would be getting dim, then dark, and he wouldn't be able to see his way home.

After another little while, he heard it again, this time closer. This confused him. It wasn't like any other noise he had ever heard. It wasn't a roar or a growl, but more like a snarl with a screech.

He was almost done, and had quite a good load of wood now to take home. The green dragon stretched and walked over to his wheelbarrow to put his last armful of wood on and prepare to leave.

Until he heard the noise again. He turned and looked around everywhere; there could be no mistake that it had come from very nearby this time, somewhere in the immediate area.

The dragon's eyes stopped scanning when he saw, coming out of the afternoon shadows of the forest, the strangest creature he had ever seen. He wasn't sure if it was aggressive, he wasn't even sure what it was, although he seemed to faintly remember some folktale of some creature that sounded like it would be similar. He instinctively grasped the handle of his ax hard.

It seemed material enough, though immaterial as well, and dragon shaped, as far as he could see. It uttered its low growl, and its eyes glowed like coals. The creature was black as night, and seemed to have the texture of roiling shadows. Stock still for a moment, it seemed to be waiting for something. Then the green dragon found out what.

Three more of its compatriots, exactly alike, stepped out from the trees, and as soon as they joined the first, the four of them leaped at him more quickly than he'd ever seen any animal move before.

If the young green dragon hadn't had his ax with him, it would have turned out a lot differently. His reflexes reacted when he saw them move, and he positioned his ax to defend himself. He struck out left and right, and hit two of them, and then struck downwards, which caught another in the head. The last one remaining, which was the one he'd first seen, was now approaching him. The young dragon swung to the side, and struck it in the left shoulder. The bit of the ax sank in, but offered little resistance to being pulled out. This last beast vanished like the others had, leaving him alone in the forest.

The green dragon turned, and quickly grabbing his wheelbarrow and pushing it away, headed for home with his load without looking back to see if any more were on the way. He hadn't gone very far into the forest, and soon reached the edge and took off across the open field beyond, with a story to tell for supper for sure. He decided to report this to the local guards tomorrow morning.

Further away from the capital, meanwhile, the guards of a garrison near the port city were preparing for the night watches, as they did every night.

The lots were being drawn for which soldier would do what post. There was the mounted guard, which rode around inside the courtyard and outside the garrison walls, as well as standing guard at the gates. Then there was the wall guard, who positioned themselves around the wall, patrolling, and watching for and challenging anyone who approached, whom they could easily see coming a great distance away.

The garrison being directly on the main road between the port and the capital, they had the responsibility of checking cargo and travelers as they passed between, and especially at night.

It was already after dark, and the guards had taken their posts, bracing themselves for what looked like another long night of checking what few travelers came by in the late hours.

The garrison crier had just called out the all's well, when in the nearby forest, unnoticed by the guards, the same creatures moved through the underbrush towards the edge of the forest, and made their way towards the garrison's walls.

The first to spot them was a mounted guard who was patrolling the side of the garrison walls nearest the forest. The creatures came up on him, and the guard barely had time to draw a weapon. They were trying to pounce on him and his horse and drag him down. Once he was on the ground, he knew it would be over.

The soldier swung his sword to keep them at bay as best he could, and his shouts attracted attention. None of the other guards who responded had ever seen anything like them either. By this time, those posted on the walls had also made their way around, and were trying to help by firing some arrows at the pack of creatures, but weren't having the best of luck due to the darkness and how well their targets blended in with it.

The guard who was attacked was now being shielded by some fellow soldiers who had spears to drive the attackers further back and keep them at bay.

This seemed to work for a while, though the creatures didn't retreat. They seemed to be staying just outside of the range of the spears, which were the longest range weapons they had. It would have been a stalemate, if one of them, seeming to be the leader, hadn't darted forth and broke the tip off of one of the spears, followed closely by the others.

It then erupted into a battle. The mounted guard drew their swords and began to slash at the beasts. It appeared that they drew strength from the darkness and shadows, for they could almost melt into them, avoiding some of the soldier's attacks.

One would disappear, and then reappear elsewhere, and when the soldiers took note of this, they knew they needed a new tactic. They had reinforcements on the way; the guards who had been positioned on the wall were coming to their aid on the ground. They were coming out of the front gates and would be arriving to assist at any moment.

One of them had gone inside the barracks to alert

the commander. The dragon had already been awakened by the noise, and was coming to investigate, when the guard caught up with him and briefed him. The commander flew up to perch on the wall to get a look at them. He had a troubled look on his face and went back inside, saying he needed to notify the guards and the king at the capital.

Outside the walls, the soldiers were slowly winning the fight. The additional troops helped to overwhelm the creatures, and they managed to dispatch some of them. The strangest thing though, was when they did, the beasts seemed to only vanish on the instant in a puff of smoke.

By the time the guards had reached the gates, with the mounted guards following, the commander had come back and called them all together to address them. He informed them that he had given proper notification and received orders in response. The mounted guard were to stay inside the walls for the rest of the night, and all of them were to remain on high alert until further notice.

At the capital, around mid morning the next day, the second hawk with the news of the victory soon arrived, and the guard who received it took it immediately to the king and his ministers. His Majesty had been awakened at the first notice, and had then ordered his ministers to be awakened as well, so as to convene with them.

The king thanked the messenger, and told him to wait while he received the information and came up with a response to send back. He broke the seal and began to read the letter.

"Your Majesty,"

CHRONICLES OF RHODRAN

"As commander, I am writing, as per my last communication, to update you on the situation in the port city garrison. The attackers were beat back, although through great effort, and barely so. I have just now spoken with the soldiers who were the first to see and counter the attackers.

They describe them as shadow beasts, with glowing eyes, deep red, and almost as flexible as fluid, somewhat solid yet difficult to attack because of their shadowy, smoky nature.

The one thing they all agree on is that they had never seen such beasts before. I can honestly say, as I was just able to catch sight of them from the ramparts of the walls, that I haven't either.

As the situation has now been resolved, I will only communicate further if further developments occur."

The king finished, and dictated a response to the effect of thanking him for the report, reiterating the order that they remain on high alert until further notice, and assuring him that extra reinforcements would be sent to his garrison. The letter also requested the commander to send the soldier who first saw the creatures so he could be privately questioned.

The hawk was sent back with the reply, and with that out of the way, the king began a serious session with all his ministers and advisers.

"Let's start with first things first," said the king, "You all tell me, in your experience, what do you think this new, shadowy threat is?"

"There's no way to tell for sure yet, Your Majesty," responded one of his highest advisers, "but it certainly reminds me of the descriptions they give in the old histories of the servants of...well, the dark dragon."

"As you say, there's no way to tell yet, but I fear you are correct." came the reply.

Just then, a guard begged entrance with another dispatch, and the king called him forth.

"This just came in," the guard explained, "from a magistrate from one of the rural provinces not far from here. He said this morning that he got a report from the son of a farmer that he had been attacked last evening."

The king took and read the report, and it did nothing to decrease the worried furrow of his brow. The description of the attackers in this case was the same as the ones at the garrison.

"This, if anything, proves beyond a doubt that these attacks were not just coincidence." he said, passing the letter around to his ministers.

Meanwhile, one asked to be excused to the archives to go look up something. He returned not much later, with a large volume, which he opened and laid on the table, and began to read a segment describing what he thought was the creature they were discussing.

"The lichs, both shadow-lichs and dragon-lichs, are creatures that are very difficult to handle with conventional weapons. They are created only by the darkest of black magic, and are loyal to whomever summoned them. They will be corporeal enough to do physical damage to any they attack, but will take little in return, with the exception of weapons that have been strengthened by enchantments or the use of a mage's magic to counter them.

The last that these malevolent and dangerous creatures were seen was during the coup attempt of the dark dragon, Laubadar. He had created them, thinking them a much better army than one of flesh and blood, as they could be nigh untiring and undying.

The vast magic of the great royal mage, Urdharmus, sealed them away afterwards, and the dragon-lichs, as they are transformed from dragons, return to normal when their master is defeated.

Both kinds of beasts are less vulnerable and more powerful during the hours of darkness. As they can literally hide in the shadows by blending in with them, they also make a tough mark, one that many an expert marksman or swordsman would be hard-pressed to strike correctly.

The beasts, even though defeated, because

undying, they will simply rise again by returning to their master and regenerating any injuries from weapon or magic. However, it does take some time to do this, so one has time to leave before any imminent danger returns."

There was, accompanying the text, a picture that looked as if it could have been drawn from the descriptions they had been given. The minister had finished reading and turned back to the king.

"Yes, it certainly does sound like what we're dealing with here...ahh, and here comes the soldier, as well, let's see what he has to say." the king said, spying that dragon coming up the throne room's carpet towards the dais where they were all seated.

The loyal guard bowed, and saluted the king. That dragon then bid him speak, and tell them what he had seen. When he had finished, the king picked up the book they had been studying.

"Did what you saw, look anything like this?" the monarch asked, showing him the picture from the book.

"Yes, your majesty, although it was harder to see it in the shadows, it looked exactly like that."

"Thank you, you're dismissed back to your post. I also request that you take this back with you." The king handed the soldier a message for the commander.

"Now that we've gotten confirmation of what it is we're dealing with," said the king, "it's high time to respond. I want increased security, especially around the capital. Shuffle soldiers around if you have to. Along with that comes the notifying the kings of the other realms." He insisted on writing it himself. A while later it was completed.

"My fellow kings,"

"I regret to inform you that the very reason we have so long been allied, so that we may join together in times of necessity, may have come to pass. I have had already two attacks on my citizens by creatures that can be none other than the lichs.

My mages now assure me that this is a bad portent, and likely foretells the resurgence of the dark dragon himself. None other than he, or at least his magic, could have conjured these beasts. If this is so, then we must brace ourselves and our realms for his return.

I am taking all precautions here, and my mages have discovered that these beasts are vulnerable to white magic. I have confidence in our chances, as Laubadar was defeated before, and I'm sure he can be again.

I will keep you updated as anything arises. Be safe, take precautions, and good luck to us all."

The king of Rhodran then had his messengers and hawks sent to the other kingdoms to warn them of the possibility of the old threat returning. He didn't want to necessarily make an immediate announcement to the citizens of his own kingdom, to avoid panicking them.

When the other kings received his news, they reacted in much the same way. There were beginning to come to them reports of these creatures lurking about in their realms as well, and they went on high alert for any more attacks, and prepared to honor their treaties with each other if necessary.

The mages were assigned to come up with a force field which would act as a shield for the capital against dark magic.

The king had the librarian bring him a specific volume from the library, a very thick tome, which contained the history of the kingdom, which might give him some insight into their current situation. If what he thought was going to happen, was really going to happen, he would need all the knowledge about it he could get. He had to prepare for the dark dragon's return.

CHAPTER ONE

Excerpt from the Chronicles of Rhodran, by the scribe

Erzadhar

Many millennia ago, we dragons shared the planet

with beings called humans. All those ages ago, we were

much different than we are now. We were not as

developed, and walked on all fours. We did not have the

capability of speech yet, nor any of the evolved powers

that we have now. We were little more than dumb

brutes. However, we were still intelligent enough to be

able to share information with each other, and the

systematic attempts at exterminating our race by the humans that had been going on for centuries had finally led them, or at least the ones that even knew of our existence at all, to believe that we were extinct.

This was, of course, not the case. We, even as we were then, knew to hide ourselves effectively enough to perpetuate this falsehood. We continued on with our societies, such as they were, while the humans remained in their set ways, all of us oblivious to what was coming.

We had at least some enjoyment out of our simple ways, and we figured that if the humans left us alone if we went into hiding, then it was worth it to do so. We had no real weapons that would work against them effectively, and as we did not wish to decimate our numbers in a futile attempt to win the fight; and could obviously see that they had no wish to negotiate, we saw no better alternatives.

However, one day, something happened to change all that. A great asteroid came, big enough to cause the extinction of many species, and so it did. The devastation was immense. Many species that had once graced the surface of this planet either disappeared immediately or, if more unfortunate, died slow deaths of starvation, whether carnivore or herbivore. The sun shone no more, so thick was the cloud cover caused by the impact. Even worse was the fact that, likely triggered by the asteroid's earth-shattering clash, some of the planet's volcanoes were seen to erupt as well.

We had no more clue that it was coming than the humans did. We did have one advantage, though, that they did not. We saw the destruction and knew that it would be a very long time before conditions would ever be able to improve enough for us to survive comfortably again. We also, being reptiles, disliked the cold that the cloud cover of ash and dirt and debris caused. We made the decision in council to go into a mass hibernation until such time as conditions did improve.

We dragons, in addition to the thick, armored hides and sharp claws that we have as reptiles, also are capable of placing ourselves into a torpor, a kind of hibernation of sorts, which allowed us to survive. We needed no food while in this state, and could remain in such state for as long as a few centuries. We hoped that by that time, despite the fact that our race, too, lost some of its members to this catastrophe, that those of us who remained would then be able to inhabit a world which would perhaps once more be hospitable to life.

We awakened to a world which had come a long way along the path to recovery. It was a world that was new and strange, and yet also familiar. Many of the plant and animal species that we had known were gone, *of course; but those that had clung stubbornly to life, as we had, seemed to amazingly be no worse for wear. It was difficult to tell that the great catastrophe had ever happened, if one did not know how the world had looked before. Despite the fact that we were glad that the world had come to heal itself, we still could not help but mourn that great loss which was all too evident to us, and to remember those of our species we lost.*

From this time, dragon-kind alone has been the alpha species of this planet. We continued for some time after as we had been, but over the generations, evolution allowed us to grow as a species and gain new abilities, now that we had no competition.

Dragons began first to evolve to stand on two feet. This has advantages over walking on all fours, as now we could begin to find and imitate the use of tools as we had seen the humans do. We had no need of some of their tools, but those we agreed were useful, we adapted to our size and abilities, and kept. Many of their ideas had to be adapted, such as armor, for human style armor would not suit us. We also had to adapt the size of a lot of other things, for the average size of a dragon is eight to ten feet tall at the shoulders, that being when standing on two legs.

Before the great catastrophe, dragons had been simpler minded, but now, with the ability to think without having to fend off a predator anymore, we improved our minds, at the same time that evolution was improving our bodies. We began to create a written language and to write down our feelings, experiences, and history, as we had seen the humans do before. This is one of the things that all dragons agree was one of the human's better ideas.

In these ways, I suppose one could say that we

carry on some aspects of the human's culture, even long after they are gone. We never did, however, adapt very many examples of what they called their "higher technology." While we did come to appreciate their arts and music, as well, and adapt those into our growing culture, we remain to this day at a level that they would have called "middle ages," although, for us at least, it is acceptable and perfectly functional with the way we organize our society.

We dragons never did have much of the independence of humans. We always were more accustomed to a social hierarchy, more akin to a lion pride. Because of the rarity of anyone protesting their place in the social scale, for the most part things always run smoothly and calmly in dragon society. For this reason, we saw no need for the complicated societies that later humans had.

A long time after these first beginnings of rebuilding our world, we noticed the first changes in our abilities that were unmistakable. Since the beginnings of our race, we have only had some abilities related to fire. However, some dragons began noticing affinities with other types of elements.

Some found that they had the ability to call the cold of the ice and snow, and to create frozen breath instead of fire. They made themselves useful to the clans by creating frost caves of ice and snow where all could store their foods and keep them cold so they would not spoil.

Others found that they had an affinity with the earth, and could not only call upon plant life to help them, but also to cause it to grow. This allowed them to help the clans by providing them with all the food they could need for their numbers.

Yet others found that they could call upon water and use it as a defense, or as a weapon. These helped the clans by assisting the frost and earth dragons in different ways. For the frost dragons, they could produce water for them, so they would have an easier time of creating their ice and snow; and for the earth dragons, they provided them water to better grow and control their plant life.

Some, of course, still retained the older powers that are shared among dragon kind, that of fire. Those continued to provide fire and warmth for the clans, as well as a good way to cook. They also tended to take the role of guards of the clans, as fire was still considered a most powerful weapon against any foes.

Every so often, there would be one born amongst us that would have scales the color of silver, and be a most unexpected surprise. These silver dragons, you see, would have one of the elemental powers, but no one would know which one until the dragon grew up.

Dragons come into their elemental abilities around the time of majority. As such, these dragons would always have to wait to find out what element they would be. It was one of these dragons that would help to change the course of dragon history.

After the differences in dragons' abilities began to show in our species, there began to be more conflicts among dragons than before. The arguments began over which of the types of dragons had the better powers. This began to break down the hierarchy that had hitherto worked so well. Some were dissatisfied with how the fire dragons seemed to still be considered more able and useful, even despite the fact that, as the elements had been abilities of our race for some time now, the others had proven their usefulness as well.

These arguments escalated into conflicts. Many on all sides felt justified, but the silver dragons sadly watched, trying to remain neutral. Just when it seemed that it was the most dire, and there would never be a solution, a silver dragon named Varthulus could stand it no longer and decided to speak up for the sake of all and end these arguments. He had an idea, and with luck, it would work.

He began by explaining that he understood that some felt undervalued in the current system, assured them that he could understand why some might feel that way, and that he had a solution to propose to them.

He continued and explained his plan. He would help to found four separate kingdoms, one for each of the different types of dragons, fire, ice, earth, and water. The current land, he thought, could be reserved for those who did not mind mingling with all the other types of dragons, and thus could be a haven for all to join together freely.

His words seemed to draw mixed reactions at first. Some seemed to like the idea, and some seemed skeptical. However, as the dragons thought about his proposal, many of them came around to his way of thinking. He worked hard to convince those who were skeptical that it could be possible to create separate living spaces for each type of dragon. He sent dragons out to find the best locations for each type.

Soon, they had located and founded areas for new kingdoms, and almost all of them were not far from the original kingdom.

The dragons of the earth migrated to a large, grassland area and founded a great, fortified city there to be their new kingdom. They settled on calling it the Kingdom of Earth, Jasmer. This kingdom agreed to handle the food supply trade for the other kingdoms, as it always had a surplus due to the earth dragons.

The fire dragons then left for a large mountainous area with a large volcano, and built their city into one of the mountains. This became Teldros, home of the fire dragons. Their great iron gates have the most intricate wrought iron carvings of any of the dragon realms. They became blacksmiths, iron workers, and soldiers for hire to the rest of the kingdoms, as these were suitable jobs for their talents.

The ice dragons departed in another direction for another mountain chain, this one full of high, snowy mountains. They carved out caves at the tops of the mountains. They called themselves the frozen ones, and named their city the same, Machdur. Their city is so full of caves, that the king himself does not even know them all, so they say. The ice dragons continued to trade in ice to the other kingdoms, and were often known to produce decent mages from their ranks.

Varthulus' scouts had found a special place for the water dragons. Although not connected to the land, they had found, a decent distance offshore, a gigantic island which would suit the water dragons perfectly. When the water dragons saw it, they agreed and soon founded their kingdom there. It was called Paledat, and had many magnificent fountains and pools for the water dragons, who would use them impressively to demonstrate their talents. They continued to provide the necessary water to the other kingdoms through trade, and settled down, in general, to scholarly pursuits.

All the remainder decided to stay in Rhodran and continue to live with the other types of dragons, as all were now welcome here. Things continued on like this for a while.

Then one day the clan of Rhodran lost its chief and leader. The leader had passed with no heirs, and so they were unsure of how to choose and who would lead. Varthulus was suggested, as a king, since the new kingdoms had chosen kings. He was extremely reluctant to accept, and at first insisted that they elect someone else to the post, but he could not sway them from their purpose.

So he was now king, and found the best advisers he could to assist him in the running of the kingdom. One of these was a mage named Urdharmus. The new ruler sensed that there was a need for magical advice and protection, and the king was indeed correct. He began his long and prosperous reign ruling wisely and fairly with their advice.

One of the old leader's advisers, Laubadar, a great black dragon, larger than any that had been seen for a long time, had been planning for a long time to take over when the old leader died, and he was most displeased with having been denied his chance. He had known for a long time that the old leader was childless, who else but he to take over? But instead, they put this young upstart on the throne, simply for solving a few petty squabbles?

Laubadar made his move. He thought it would be over quickly due to his size against the young ruler's, but failed to account for the difference in strength due to the difference in age. The young king prevailed, though injured. He gave the decree of banishment for treason against the king, and Laubadar swore vengeance on him and his line.

Urdharmus knew this was no idle threat. He also

knew Laubadar was unlikely to attempt the same thing twice, and so he knew measures must be taken to prepare for the unexpected when he did return.

With the king's permission and understanding, the great mage began his preparations to secure the kingdom against Laubadar's return. He began by inspecting the soldiers, especially the royal guards, to see what could be done to make them more ready. He came up with the idea of producing special magical collars that could protect them from at least some of Laubadar's magic. Next he enhanced their armor by adding his magical spells for protection.

Then he turned his attention to what exactly might be needed to prevent being taken by surprise. He enacted a spell that placed a protective area all around the capital, which would allow him to detect any trace of Laubadar entering the city. He also told his informants to be alert and notify him the moment they saw anything of any note whatsoever.

The wait didn't last very long. Soon enough, there were heralds bringing news about the fall of the ice kingdom, with all the others soon after. It was all too apparent who the next target would be. The king was in near constant council with his advisers, and his court mage most of all. The flow of refugees fleeing their homes headed straight for the capital of Rhodran, and resulted in small refugee camps within the walls of the city, between houses, in alleys, anywhere they could fit.

The kings of the displaced kingdoms had also fled to plead for assistance. They were invited to stay in the palace until such time as they could be placed back on their rightful thrones by the defeat of the black dragon and his armies. They promised use of what remained of their armies towards the defense of the city and *everyone taking refuge there.*

The most disturbing thing that came to be known through these reports, was that while some had fled and escaped, Laubadar had captured some from the other realms, and those he had captured he had used dark magic to transform into dragon-lichs, undead armies at his sole command.

Not too many days after, near daybreak, the guards did indeed see the great army coming. It was more than anyone could have expected. Laubadar came at the head of many thousands of his undead soldiers.

The forces seemed so vast as to stretch across the horizon. Fortunately, since the dark dragon's coming had been known before, albeit not knowing exactly his force's numbers, which gave a chance for Urdharmus to study how to counter it. He fortified the defenses and began to work on a spell to reverse the dark magic once Laubadar was defeated.

The guards remained on alert and began the battle when the army arrived at the gates. They used the defenses of boulders, molten metal and boiling water. Laubadar tried to get around this by sending some of his dragon-lichs to try to fly above, but this was turned back by catapults knocking them out of the sky. They didn't stay down for long, but the guards were able to keep them out of commission for long enough periods of time that they were still unable to get past the city walls and gates.

Meanwhile, both Laubadar and Urdharmus were working to cast spells to fortify their own sides respectively. The battle continued for days, but it became obvious that the dragon-lichs would not tire, whereas eventually the guards would. They had already been changing shifts to work the walls and catapults to avoid tiring.

The battle ended only when Urdharmus came forward, having completed his counter spell to deal with the threat of Laubadar. The two mages had a short, but powerful one-on-one battle, with a back and forth exchange of spells, firing through the night with vivid colors and sounds. The guards had long ago withdrawn out of the immediate area to avoid being caught in the crossfire.

Soon enough, Laubadar was kneeling, panting, and at Urdharmus' sole mercy. Urdharmus knew it would be folly to allow him to simply leave and recover his strength and regroup his army. He had been working on a special spell to imprison him and end his threat, hopefully for good.

He droned the incantation in his deep, low voice. Soon all that were watching could see a crystalline cage of webbing forming around the black dragon. A few more moments and it began to solidify between the webs and then solidify into crystal, forming a strong prison around him. Next, although all this happened quicker than it seemed, the crystal began to shrink and the black dragon inside began to shrink with it. A very short time later, a regular sized red crystal was laying on the floor, with a shadowy imprint of the black dragon the only thing that remained of him.

The old mage who had defeated his foe slowly walked up and picked up the crystal. The only response it made was the throbbing glow that it seemed to emit continuously anyway, and nothing else. The battle was over. Peace had been secured once again.

The tired old dragon mage knew that the next step

must be to deal with the dragon-lichs that the Laubadar had created. He began to recite the counter spell that he had come up with, and prayed that he had done everything correctly.

When the spell was done, all of the dragons that had been transformed into dragon-lichs were back to normal, and the final skirmishes were ended. Many of the dark dragon's followers were imprisoned, but some had fled and were never found.

The five kings then sat in council, to determine how to rebuild and what to do now. They agreed that they would send a team, consisting of the best of all the kingdom's builders and artisans, to each kingdom in turn, until all of them were rebuilt and thriving again.

Meanwhile, the old mage had decisions of his own to make. The first was, what to do with the crystal that now contained Laubadar?

There was no way that it could just be left out in the open, or even stored away somewhere in the castle. That left too much to chance, and the risk that one of Laubadar's followers could resurface and try to release him was too great. No, a different hiding place would have to be found, one that would be protected by his spells, and chosen so that it would likely never be located.

And then there was the issue of what to do with the powerful objects he had created, and where to hide them. The royal mage knew that these could not be placed near the crystal, as that would make it too easy for someone else to both release Laubadar to get rid of his only obstacle once and for all.

Eventually, he must have made his decisions, as,

although it was never publicly confirmed, he and his apprentice went on missions which must have been to seal away the crystal and the objects, as none of them were ever seen again afterward in the realm of Rhodran.

The great royal mage passed away soon after, and so it is likely that none will ever know of the location where any of these currently resides, but the mage did give some advice to the kings of the realms that they should have a backup plan in case Laubadar should return, as even he could not be entirely sure that the barrier could hold such a dragon, proficient in dark magic as he was, forever. There was also no telling if the seal itself would wear over time. No such seal had ever been attempted on a living being before. It might last a week; on the other hand, it might last centuries.

As the efforts to clean up and repair the realms

began to get underway, peace and the rule of law seemed to once again settle over the kingdoms.

However, despite the fact that the rebel dragon and his armies had been stopped, the kingdoms were still new. The kings decided that, in hopes of preventing another occurrence of the rebellion, that there needed to be some voice for the citizens that could help bring any complaints to light and assist in resolving them before the dissatisfaction boiled over into open conflict, as it had here.

So, the kings created, in each realm, a council to have members that were chosen by the citizens of that realm, which would have the power to bring up any grievances to the king. Representatives from each realm would also meet once a year to smooth out the relations between realms.

They also strengthened their alliances by choosing the kings of Rhodran to be the high kings of the realms, and made treaties of alliance in case any realm was attacked. This was to make it harder for Laubadar to recapture all the realms, if he should return, or any others that might follow on that path.

The rebuilding of the realms proceeded apace, and soon it was difficult to tell that the rebellion had happened and such damage had been done. The walls of Rhodran alone had several large breaches that had to be hand repaired to secure them again. That, however, was not the least of it, and the other realms, especially the ice realm, had much work to be done before things were back to normal.

Although it has been many long years since these events, and many have long since forgotten the legends of these early days of the dragon realms, there are some who have not forgotten the first great royal mage's warnings, and that the possibility still exists that the great black dragon could break the seal and return someday...

CHAPTER TWO

2,500 years later...

The sun began to slowly rise on the capital city of the realm of Rhodran, which was called Cordaru. For a capital, the city seemed sleepy enough, although if one looked closely enough, one could tell that many of the city's multitudinous inhabitants were already awake. Lights were on early in many of the small shops, such as the baker, and the book printer's shop. These were already hard at work, although dawn had barely arrived. Some early risers peeped their heads out of their doors to see the first shafts of sunlight come over the city walls, and pour down the streets in beams of light.

The great city itself was certainly worthy of some moments of study and reflection. The great outer wall that had stood for many millennia to keep out anyone who was not wanted was but one of the city's many amazing sights. As one passed by, one could hear the shouts of the guards who patrolled the top of the walls as they passed from one guard post to another, solemn faces seeming to never change as they performed their duties and protected those inside.

Many of the castle guards also patrolled the streets, at least those that did not have other duties. One could always notice them; they stuck out in a crowd. How could they not, considering that they were the only dragons besides the nobles allowed to wear armor? And not just any armor, either, the special armor that they had traditionally worn ever since the days of the first king.

It was a brilliant, shining silver, with special fitted helmets to allow the dragon soldier's horns to come through without catching inside. They also carried a spear and sword at their sides. The breastplates that they wore bore the king's crest, and on the captains and officers, their arm guards did too.

The crest was in the shape of a diamond, with four other diamonds pointing straight out from each of the center diamond's sides. The whole effect was almost like that of a star. It was meant to represent his high-kingship over the other realms, as well as their unity. The king's crest wasn't solely on the armor, however. It was on everything from the public buildings to the palace.

The king's palace was easily one of the most impressive and largest buildings in the city. It stood nearly as tall as the walls, and had long been the refuge of last resort. No wonder during the attack of Laubadar many centuries ago, that all who escaped him had fled there in the hope that it would not be breached, even if the walls were.

In one of these many twisting and turning hallways, always having soft carpets and rugs running along the floors of each corridor, up some stairs that had long rung with the echoes of many generations of feet padding along them, and far up one of the many towering turrets that the castle and palace boasted, there was a room, finely appointed with all sorts of plush furniture and exquisitely woven tapestries, and inside a lone figure slept away, oblivious to the stirrings of life all around in the city below.

No less oblivious was she to the fact that there was a chambermaid making her way up the stairs to awaken her to begin her day.

"Your Highness? Princess? Princess?" said the chambermaid, calling her mistress after the customary knock at her chamber door.

The young adult, female silver dragon, large for her age, grumbled slightly and debated whether to turn over or start to wake up.

"Princess?" came the call again.

"Yes, yes, I'm awake." the sleepy dragon replied. The silver dragon pushed off her covers and swung her hind legs over the side of the bed.

She was of a uniform silver coloration for her scales, with harder, white belly scales from the tip of her tail to her neck, which all dragons had, and that acted as a natural armor. She stretched her arms, then her wings, and refolded them to her sides. She stood up on her two hind legs and walked over to let in the waiting chambermaid.

"Princess Asvartha," said her chambermaid as soon as the door had been opened, "we have to hurry. You know you have the meeting with the council today."

"Yes, I know," the princess replied, "but they still won't tell me what it's all about."

"Well, let's get you ready and I suppose you'll find out soon enough."

The chambermaid busied herself to gather the necessary things for the princess's morning routine, and soon had her white mane brushed and her jewelry adorning her: the princess had golden anklets and armlets, as well as a necklace with a pendant, all bearing the royal crest, of course.

"Don't forget your diadem, too." The chambermaid placed the circlet of gold over the silver female's horns and down on her head.

"Now, you better head on and hurry to the council meeting, they spoke as if this would be something very important."

The princess thanked her, and started down the stairs to leave the palace and head to the Council House a couple of blocks away.

The crowds in the streets had also begun to gather, as this was a public meeting and all were invited.

Fortunately, the Great Council House was, if anything, very hard to miss. It was a great gray stone building, roofed with wood; which most public houses were, as compared with private residences, which were thatched instead.

Inside the building, the council members, of all types and both genders, had begun to gather for the meeting. They wore long, flowing robes as a mark of their positions, and the head members of the council served as the king's advisers.

The council hall itself had seats enough for all the council members, and there were a few hundred of them, the high council members being on the dais in front. The reason the council house was a three story building, however, was the two great galleries, one above the other on the top two stories, which allowed the citizens to see the meetings.

The council members, as was typical, were already

having discussions among themselves before the meeting started.

"Do you suppose the others we've invited will show?" asked a red dragon female to a colleague.

"I suppose we'll see." the blue dragon male answered. "I certainly hope so. After all, they're going to need..."

They were cut off by the Council Leader, a large red dragon named Rorzkar calling them to order to start the meeting in a few minutes.

Meanwhile, a young male blue dragon made his way through the crowd to the council. He was relatively young, about the princess's age, and had dark blue scales, lighter blue belly scales, and a dark mane with pointy ears and horns. He wondered why on earth they had invited him. Perhaps some question that they needed scholarly advice on? After all, that was his forte. He pushed his glasses up on his face and clutched his invitation as he prepared to enter past the guards.

Two other dragons also were heading to the main chamber, having been invited.

"Why do you reckon we were called here?" asked the first, a male green dragon. He had green scales, with black belly scales and mane, and fanned ears, with no horns on his head.

"Not sure about you, but I know why I'm here." the second responded, a red dragon dressed in armor, obviously a knight of the realm. This one had red scales, with yellow belly scales, a white mane and pointed ears and horns.

"Oh, yeah? Why?"

"Because," said the dragon knight, "my father's the Council Leader, and obviously he has some important mission for me to do for the council."

"If you're so good on your own, then why send for others?" the green dragon retorted.

The dragon knight's response, if he was going to make any, was preempted by the guard calling them forward into the chambers.

The final invited dragon was also there, making her way through the crowds to the council chambers. This dragoness was turquoise green in her coloration, with darker green belly scales and a brown mane, with fanned ears and no horns. The green female dragon, a mage, suspected that they wanted her advice on some aspect of magic. If that was so, she would be more than happy to assist them and the royal family in any way she could.

These four, and indeed all the townsfolk who had come to the meeting, could not resist craning their necks upward to view the great chamber of the council. It was paneled all around the chamber from floor to ceiling in rich, dark wood. The floors were of smooth stone, with a great aisle leading down the two sides of seats where the council sat. If one looked up as one entered, one could see the ceiling, decorated with scenes of dragon history. The two balconies, which had banisters of dark wood and were accessible by staircases on the left and right of the entrance, were a sight to behold as well, particularly when they were packed with spectators as they were today.

Soon, everyone, including the princess, had arrived and was seated. The four other dragons that had been called specifically were seated in the front row with the princess occupying her father's seat in the dais. It seemed that the entirety of the great, wood paneled room turned in unison towards the dais as the high council sat down and the council leader stood up to address the room.

"Now," boomed the voice of Council Leader Rorzkar, over the crowd's murmuring, which immediately silenced them. "It's high time we got started with this meeting. I'm sure you're all curious as to why we called all of you here this morning."

Whispers once again ran through the crowd.

"Well, let me tell you bluntly. We're here to discuss the disappearance of the king, and what needs to be done."

The crowd now listened intently. There had indeed been rumors lately that the king had gone off on a quest, and had gone missing, something to do with the recent upsurge of happenings connected with dark magic.

"The rumors are true. There have been coming to us, even as late as yesterday, reports from the other realms about sightings of dragon-lichs, which of course have not been seen since the days of the black dragon, Laubadar. That's not all, either. There are other instances which the royal wizards, including the grand wizard, assure the council could only be the result of black magic."

The entire crowd reacted with murmurs of shock, and he paused to let it sink in.

"The king did indeed hear these reports months ago, and then two months ago, he left to see if there was anything he could do. It would seem that, as we have not heard from him in several weeks now, he may have been captured, or at least is missing."

The princess had known that her father had gone off, much as he had before, and had suspected that it was for that reason, but still... She had of course, heard the rumors as well as anyone else, but to have such a thing confirmed...

"I know, princess, that this must be at least somewhat of a shock. The king requested his ministers to tell no one, on account of giving away his plans, or in your case, causing you unnecessary worry, as it was still possible that he would succeed."

"However," he continued, "it has become apparent that he has at least met some...difficulties in this task, and as such we must move on to his other instructions that he left us."

"He had been studying a book, one which had been written during the time of the first king, on what might be able to assist us should the great black dragon return from his imprisonment."

One of the crowd could stand it no longer and blurted out: "So, what did he find? Is Laubadar coming back? How do we stop him?"

"I'm coming to that," replied the Council Leader calmly. "When he left, the king did send some letters keeping us up to date with his quest. It is because these letters have stopped completely that we fear that he is captured. His last letter gave some...interesting findings. He said that he had journeyed to where the crystal containing Laubadar was hidden, and that it appeared that the force field was weakening, although not yet breached."

Being met with silence, he continued, "He also said that he had deciphered the fact that, if he should fail, and Laubadar should come back, that the only one who could do so would be one of his bloodline."

"The princess!" everyone gasped and called in unison.

"Yes, the princess," Rorzkar said, "and although he regretted it being the only choice, he stated that if the time came for her to set out on the quest in his stead, that he did not wish her to go alone, and indeed, she might need other assistance rather than going on a lone mission."

"That is why I have called these other four here today. Each of them will have a part to play in the princess's guard. He wanted her to have the best chance of success, especially because, if she must go, it means he had failed, and he had underestimated the threat level to a lone dragon."

Now the blue dragon who had been invited spoke up: "But why us, in particular? What do we have that she needs?"

"I'm coming to that, too," said the Council Leader. "You four were chosen, simply put, for your skill sets that might be needed."

"Skill sets?" questioned the small blue dragon.

"Yes. You, Rordgur, for instance, are a scholar. Very useful for deciphering and translating in the field when something comes up. When you are dealing with something that is that ancient, you never know what kind of writings you might encounter."

"As for my son, Horzkar, he's the guardian and

soldier of the group. It's likely not going to be easy going, especially if what we suspect is true."

Turning to the female green dragon, he said, "You, Targarma, were chosen for your tremendous magical potential in the academy, and thus will be handy for providing the explanation for and assisting with the resolution of any magical phenomenon, and also providing offensive magic, if necessary."

Turning at last to the green male dragon, he continued on: "And finally you, Eordwar. You might not have, well let's just say, the cleanest record, but as a well-known rogue you might have abilities and connections that could prove quite useful. We are willing to look the other way during this mission, and wipe the slate clean upon successful completion if you participate. Agreed?"

"Agreed," the green dragon replied.

The meeting was then adjourned, with the Council Leader promising the citizens that the expedition would be underway as soon as feasible. However, when the group turned to leave, he requested them to enter into his private office for a further briefing.

"Now that we have the official meeting out of the way, we can get down to the other matters at hand." the red dragon sighed, the fact of having to be the temporary decision maker obviously taking its toll.

"There's more?" asked Eordwar.

"Of course. At a minimum, we have arrangements to make for you to leave."

"Oh, right."

"There's also the matter of what I didn't want to

reveal in the public meeting. The king did not take the book with him, he left it here, and his instructions indicated to give it to you and your group, princess."

So saying, he produced an ornate volume, a seemingly ancient tome. It had dark, black leather covers, embossed with the seal of the realm on the back cover, and a dragon with open wings on the front cover. It had metal triangular sheathes on each corner of the front and back covers, and a large red ribbon for a bookmark.

On his desk, there were also a bundle of papers, which the princess noted seemed to be in her father's handwriting. These seemed to be notes of some sort related to the book. She also noted that they seemed to be unusually messy and hurriedly written.

"This," explained Rorzkar, pointing to the volume,

"is the journal of the great mage Urdharmus, the mage of the first dragon king, Varthulus. In this book, he wrote down all his research on Laubadar and all possible ways that could defeat or imprison this threat. This very book, princess, is what your father was studying so intently, in the hopes of finding some way to do just that, as he strongly suspected the dark one's return."

The princess spoke up. "And, did he find anything?"

"Yes, he found this." He indicated a page on a special gauntlet and spear that had been fabricated by the great mage long ago. "According to what the king found, the mage left these behind for anyone who might have to face Laubadar again, should the seal on him weaken and return him to the realms."

"Does it say where to find it?"

"No, likely for safety's sake. However, the king's notes that he left here say that he seemed to decipher how to find out: you have to go to the seer, and ask her the path to finding them."

"There's yet another matter to discuss, and it pertains to you, princess."

"Me? What do you mean?"

"Your father also left me another paper, a letter, and instructed me to give this to you, as it is intended for you alone."

She took the envelope with the familiar handwriting from him, and thanked him before stepping out of the room to read it. She sat down and opened it, quickly breaking the seal, wanting to commit this message to memory.

"*Dearest Daughter,*" the letter began,

"I wanted to take some time to write this to you before I have to leave for my journey. I hope that I will be successful and return home soon, but just in case I'm not, I have some things I want to share with you.

By the time you will have received this letter, I know you will have heard the whole situation from my Council Leader, so I won't go over that again. Instead, I will give you some advice that I wish I had more time before to give you.

I know you are yet young, very young. If you should have to take over the reins of the kingdom from me, and face that burden, know that I want you to know that you don't have to do everything alone. That is part of why I want you to go with this group that has been chosen for you. A monarch will tire quickly if he or she tries to run an entire kingdom on his or her own. This is why I want you to have this experience, to show you how to choose those who have talents which they can use together for the good of all.

I believe that I should be able to resolve this situation alone, however, if that should fail, the only other option is a group mission. When you were left as my heir, I had more desire than ever to protect you. There are no other options, however, as it must either be me or one of my bloodline. This is yet another reason why I must attempt this now, before it comes to that.

I hope you have been following my advice and learning and observing your mother closely. She will teach you everything you need to know about being a good monarch. Every voice in a kingdom should be heard, that is what the job of the monarch is all about.

I hope sincerely that you will never have to read this, and that I can complete my mission safely and return soon. If that is not the case, though, I want you to know that I have the utmost faith that you will complete the mission that I have not, and afterwards will be able to rule in my stead, and that I am always proud of you.

Thinking of you always,

Your father, King Valwardus

As she finished reading, she folded up the letter and went back inside the Council Leader's chambers.

"Did you learn anything new?" asked the Council Leader.

"No, it was a private letter."

"Well, now that you're back, as I was just explaining to them, since the seer lives on an island near the water realm, we will be chartering a ship to carry you there, from the sea port of Avarthu."

"But why not just take one of the royal ships?" asked the scholar.

"Well, that is one option, however, as we are aiming for the utmost stealth possible, it seems best to go for the less obvious option, to conceal as far as possible that this is an official mission."

"Well, I suppose that's true. We don't want to come out of the gate letting everyone know what we're doing."

"Indeed you don't." replied the Council Leader. "Especially as you could easily be trailed by enemy actors, or even worse. No, it's best to play it safe when we aren't even sure whether or not Laubadar has broken the seal yet. Announcing what you're doing in that case would be putting targets on yourselves."

The meeting dragged on, late into the evening, and covered a variety of strategies and other information. Before dismissing them, the Council Leader handed the princess a pouch of coins.

"This is the funds for this mission. Since expenses for such missions are difficult to calculate beforehand, we were more on the generous side, to ensure you had what you needed."

Then he turned back to the whole group.

"Now, remember, all of you, I want you to pack up and return here for one last thing tomorrow morning as soon as you are done, and then you head to the port to catch your ship."

The five dragons left the Council Leader's chambers

and went their separate ways. The princess flew back to the palace and entered past the guards at the gates.

She knew it must be past dinner time by now, and due to the meeting having made her skip lunch, she was very hungry.

When she arrived down the first floor's large corridors to the main dining hall, she saw that it was indeed dinner time, and she only hoped she hadn't missed it.

The great dining hall stretched out before her, many long, wooden tables being set with several courses of delicious looking food. It could be simply because she was very hungry, but tonight, it seemed more sumptuous than ever.

The nobles who dined here were all sitting in their places at the tables, with luxuriant capes and bejeweled breastplates adorning them, showing that these were no dragons of ordinary rank.

A servant came over to her and led her to her seat, and made sure that she got all the food that had been saved for her, and that it was still warm. She ate everything, and soon had satiated her appetite. She wasn't sure if it was all the food, or the events of the day, but soon she was almost overcome with sleepiness, and had them clear her food, and left to head up to her bedroom.

The princess, more tired than she'd ever remembered being in a long time, climbed the familiar path up the stairs to her room. She was glad to find herself in front of her door at last. She was so eager to get some rest, that she didn't even ring up her chambermaid to help her. In a very short time, she had her jewelry off, and had laid her head on her pillows.

She drifted off to sleep, thinking of all that had happened today, and all there was to do tomorrow.

CHAPTER THREE

Two Months Earlier...

The court was busier, it seemed, than it had ever been. The king, currently sitting on his throne in the grand throne room of the palace, which had been ruled by his family for centuries now, was also hard at work, along with the best scholars, mages, and advisers that his kingdom could offer.

The great silver dragon, adorned with gold and jewels of all types, and wearing a circlet crown which his horns elegantly curved back around, and a cape around his shoulders which trailed behind him, sat in a pose more befitting a thinker than a noble or a king. His eyes were concentrating on a book in front of him, though his mind began to wander.

For a few weeks now, reports had been reaching his kingdom of things that were...or should be...impossible. There was no way that such things could happen...or at least, not unless the unthinkable had happened, and the great dark dragon had returned, or was returning.

So, in light of the danger, the king had secretly ordered that all possible methods of finding out what was going on and taking steps against any threats were to proceed apace until a solution was found. Many of the scholars and mages here had been up for several nights in an attempt to find any scrap of help, or a hint from any source they could think of.

The great chamber and audience room, usually full of citizens, come to plead the king's favor for one thing or another, or else to ask his help and judgment, was very different now. The king could almost not suppress a small chuckle at what a sight it looked now.

Many scribes and scholars had books and papers all around them on the many tables that had been brought in to aid in this endeavor. Some of them even had spread out on the floor. It looked more like he'd let the local university's students in for a study session than a large, important, and very serious research project.

The king shook his head to clear his thoughts, and ending his reveries, he returned his focus to the task at hand.

Currently, he was carefully reading through the

notes of the successor to the first royal mage. He thought that perhaps there he might find some clue as to where he could find some help. The first royal mage had defeated Laubadar, after all, and perhaps his successor knew something about how and where he might have left something, anything, that could help someone else defeat him again.

He turned back to the book and began reading the notes.

"My esteemed predecessor, the first great royal mage, Urdharmus, even as the enemy armies were at the very gates of the city, was still at a loss as to how to put an end to Laubadar's reign of terror. He continued to rack his brain while he provided magical buffers to the soldiers on the front lines. His patience was rewarded, however, when his gaze fell upon the cage of an old pet bird of his, and this sparked an idea.

Laubadar was nigh-invulnerable, and so would be very difficult to kill. Besides this, the mage did not particularly want to have to kill him, unless absolutely necessary. Some would argue that it was already, but he still loathed the idea.

So instead, he contrived to bring Laubadar's ambitions to a halt using a two part plan: first, in addition to the buffers he had given the kingdom's knights, he would create for them all special magical collars, which would cancel out the effects of the black dragon's dark magic. The second part would be to battle and weaken him, and then create a magical cage of sorts to imprison him, hopefully for all eternity.

With this plan in place, he studied how to bring it about. Soon he had created the collars, and thereafter had them distributed to the soldiers.

Then he quickly created a strong spell that would entrap Laubadar and reduce him to simply an essence sealed in a crystal. To enact the spell, he created a special magical gauntlet and spear which would first weaken his opponent, allowing him to trap him.

The story of their battle is known by all and sundry, but there was a bit more to the aftermath than what is generally known.

The great mage, my mentor, having secured the kingdom's safety, did think on what to do to ensure that such spells and objects were properly kept out of sight. He did not simply want to leave it to chance that another with bad intentions could try to use them against innocents, or destroy them to enable the dark dragon's return. He finally decided to hide them away, sealed just as Laubadar was. He also decided to hide his book of notes as well. This book contains the only clues to finding the gauntlet and the spear's location. To further ensure that it would be difficult to reunite them, he hid the book and the objects separately.

Not long after, being of great age, and due to the strain that using such strong magic placed on him, my mentor passed, and I became the new royal mage. I myself was never made privy to the information of where the objects are hidden, however, I do know that the book was hidden in the mage's private magic lab where he had trained me, hidden in an underground cave deep in the middle of the forest outside of the city."

Here! This was what he had been looking for!

The king called over one of his mages to help him verify whether or not this information could be valid. It was confirmed that the archives had accepted this volume from the student of the first royal mage, and so in all likelihood, the information was valid.

The king decided to tarry no longer, and leave as soon as possible to search for the location of the first royal wizard's notes. If he could find them, then these should shed further light on what to do about their current situation.

The king ordered his horses saddled and brought forth as quickly as possible. He wasn't going to go in the carriage, nor with a large group, as he didn't want this mission to be general knowledge. The only companion for this mission was a mage, so that any enchantments or seals on the cave lab could be broken. It would be unlikely that, after all that precaution, the royal mage would have left the place unprotected by magic to keep out unwanted visitors.

He and the mage made good time, but were forced

to camp for the night when sundown came. They continued on the next day, and with the mage's help, found the location of the cave that held the mage's lab.

The cave entrance was large, but they could tell that it was only an entrance chamber as they held up their torches for light. Near the back, they saw a passageway leading further back. After following this for a while, they encountered a seal, and the mage confirmed that this meant they were going the right way.

Soon enough, they entered the cave lab of the first royal mage. It was simple enough, as the king looked around, he saw a few tables with vials, bottles, books and papers. On shelves high above, he saw candles and other accouterments, both magic and mundane. From the sheer amount of dust and spider webs he saw, he concluded it was likely that the place hadn't been used since the book had first been hidden here. He didn't know which of the books here might be the one they were looking for, but he started to search through them for ones that seemed promising.

At last the mage found the volume they were looking for, and soon enough, they were back in the palace with their prize, and the king and the mages were all trying to decipher the text.

Although the royal mages had made temporary magical copies of the book so that everyone could study it at the same time, the progress was still slow. The king grew concerned that in the meantime, the reports were still coming in of mysterious goings-on and even more mysterious sightings of creatures that met the description of dragon-lichs.

However, one of the mages soon found a clue: the

name of a former associate of Urdharmus, who was a blue dragon, and a seer. He had been the one to help the great mage to see and thwart the rebellion of Laubadar through his prophecies.

The king thought on this, and had them do further research to find if this seer had any descendants yet living who might have his powers, and provide the same service.

Upon the research coming back that there were descendants, and locating one of them on a small island of the coast of the water realm island, the king made his decision. He would need to quickly get to this seer and find out from her the location of the gauntlet and spear.

Of course, that was assuming she was willing to do so in the first place, and that she knew the location, or knew how to get it. But then, he in his turn was more than willing to pay very handsomely for any information that she might have, no matter how seemingly small.

As the rest of his preparations for a very long journey were getting underway, he then summoned his council to him. He had a great many things to discuss, and more to arrange for in case they should be necessary. He made sure to tell them his full plans, and what to do should he be captured or worse. He then handed the Council Leader two letters, one with the written version of the instructions that he had just given them, to confirm that they were his wishes, and another that he insisted be given to his daughter should it seem that he might not come back.

His further instructions for the council, in the worst case scenario that both he and the dragons sent on the later mission should fail, were to prepare the guards and the citizens of the town to hold the walls for as long as was possible. Laubadar would likely win if they couldn't find what they were looking for, but there was no reason to make it easy for him. Everyone in town was to do their part to ensure that his armies were kept at bay for the greatest amount of time.

The last thing he needed to do before he left was to inform his wife and his daughter. He wound his way through the palace halls and had a short discussion with his wife to let her know that she would be acting as regent. She didn't need detailed information or assistance at all, she had several times before been his regent while he was away or unavailable for any reason. He had the utmost faith in her, that she would govern just as well as he could in his stead.

The only thing that truly bothered him was what and how he was going to tell his daughter. Oh, he knew that she had seen him go off before, and that she was a young adult now, but he had truly never gone off on a mission before that there was a possibility that he would not return.

As he walked towards her room, he contemplated what to say. He decided that, for her own safety, he could not tell her exactly what he was doing. He had not told the queen, either, for that matter, only that she would be regent. It was better that way. If the worst happened to him, they wouldn't have any information that Laubadar would need to get out of them.

He soon approached the familiar door, and knocked to let her know he was there.

"Come in." came the response.

Oh, good, she's here, he thought.

He opened the door and entered. The princess had

turned her head at hearing the door open.

"Oh, hello, father." She said at the sight of him.

"Hello, dear. I've come to let you know that I'll be leaving soon, and that your mother will take care of things while I'm gone."

"Oh, okay. How long do you plan on being gone?"

"That's the thing. I'm not sure. Although I know your mother can handle things for me here, I'm not sure how long this will take. It could take a long time."

"Actually," he spoke up again after a pause, "that's kind of the other thing I wanted to talk to you about. You've been trained in royal protocol, laws, history, and all that for a long time now, right?"

"Of course, ever since I can remember. Why?"

"If this turns out to take longer than expected, I

want you to carefully observe your mother and how she does the day-to-day royal business. You need to have as much experience as you can with the finer points of the things a monarch does. That way you'll be better prepared for when you have to take over."

"Dad, you know that's probably not going to be for a long time, now."

"Well, I hope so, but one can never tell. That's why I want you to be as prepared as possible when it does."

"Okay, I promise."

"All right. Now, I've got to get ready to go. Make sure to help your mother as much as you can, and I hope to be back sooner rather than later."

He took his leave of her and went to pack. It seemed as though all necessary things to handle affairs in the kingdom had been arranged, and now was the time to leave.

Soon enough, he and his mage were flying towards the sea port, and soon after, were underway on the ship towards the seer's island.

They were able to convince her to have a meeting with them by overcoming her test. She proved herself more than willing to reveal information to help him, and he headed off to the spot she indicated for further investigation.

He remembered her words, and thought of them as he traveled on to the next location. She had handed him a map, and given him a prophecy:

"You yourself will not likely be the one to defeat Laubadar, however, you can investigate and find information that will be useful once passed on to those who will. For this reason, I am giving you this map. It was given to my ancestors by the royal mage, Urdharmus, who told us to give it to the one who would find out if Laubadar's seal was truly broken. This is the only clue he left to where he sealed away the crystal with Laubadar in it. We were even told strictly never to break the seal on the map."

Although he was shocked by her assertion that there was little he could do to stop the black dragon if he should return, the two travelers decided that the best thing to do was to heed her advice and go check the imprisoning crystal. That would settle any doubts about what was going on.

They took the ship, and were soon back to the mainland. He had opened the map, and it indicated an old, large tree in the middle of the snowy forest in the ice kingdom.

They stopped to get permission to enter and venture to check on the crystal from the ice realm's king. Permission was soon granted, and they flew off to their destination from there.

The snow-covered trees looked picturesque as they flew over them, and none so much as their target: a mighty oak, likely having stood for hundreds of years, and seen many snows such as this before. They landed, and the sound of the snow beneath their feet seemed the only sign of life for many miles around.

The mage got to work disarming the protective spells so they could inspect the crystal, and the king, when he was done, looked to see where in the tree the crystal might be hidden. He spied a hollow in the tree, a fair ways up the trunk.

He climbed up, and peered inside to see the

condition of the prison of the great dark dragon. When he had satisfied himself as to what the situation looked like, he climbed back down.

"Well," he reported to the mage, "It appears that the crystal is intact for now, but it does appear to have a crack. I'm not much on magic, but that concerns me."

"As well you should be, and as am I. If the condition of the seal that holds Laubadar in the crystal has deteriorated enough that it has cracked, it won't be long before he might be able to escape it completely."

"So what do you propose we do? Is there anything we can do here?"

"Keep an eye on it. As the seal breaks, the cracks will grow. When they start to spider web out, we will know he is about to break free. As for right now, we need to inform the ice realm's king, in particular, to have his men on high alert."

"Is there no way to repair the seal or recast the spell?"

"No, sealing spells are notoriously difficult, and even more so those that try to entrap a living being. That's the reason why it took so long, even for the great royal mage, to come up with a spell that would be effective. The only way to recast the spell is to wait until the seal breaks and frees the thing that was sealed, and then recast it. As you can imagine, with a living being, especially in this case, that will prove difficult."

"Although," he continued, "all hope may not yet be lost. That's why I suggest that we stay nearby. If we catch it quick enough when the seal first breaks, I might be able to recast the spell and recapture Laubadar, but that might be a long shot."

The king had soon made his decision. "For now, let's do as you suggest and go warn the ice realm's king, and send some news back with our ship to our realm and the others. Then we can come back here and set up camp nearby to keep watch on things here."

As they left, the glow that surrounded the crystal prison, and the shadow within that was the remnant of the dark dragon, seemed to increase, almost as if the malice contained within could sense that the time of its release was near.

They flew back over the mountains that rung the valley around the snowy forest, and back to the magnificent palace of the ice realm's dragon king.

They warned him, and as they advised, he did indeed place every available soldier of his realm on high alert for any signs of the rise of the ancient enemy.

The king quickly wrote out letters to his council and the other realm's kings, and sent his ship on its way to deliver them. By the time they were done with this, they notified the ice realm's king that they would be returning to monitor the situation.

They stayed long enough to ensure that the ice realm's king, Karvarthuk, had put his men on their guard, and then traveled back to the forest to camp nearby.

Once the two had checked on the crystal when they returned, then they began to look for a place that would be suitable and protected enough for a long term stay, if it came to that. They cleared and expanded an ice cave that they came upon nearby and set up camp there. Neither had any clue how long they were going to have to be there. They agreed they would be checking on the crystal every day to see the progress, or if there was any.

The first few days were uneventful. The mage had been casting spells to make the seal last a bit longer, and make it take longer to break completely, but even those would not hold forever.

They had brought weapons from the ice realm palace in case they were faced with a situation where they might need them.

Valwardus looked around their makeshift camp. The slick ice walls shone around him, and all manner of things were strewn on the floor. Their bedrolls were rolled out on the ice floor, and on the mage's side, many books and papers were on top of his temporary bed.

As for Valwardus himself, he was in charge of making sure the fire stayed lit. The mage had said that shadowy versions of dragon-lichs might start to appear, and fire was one thing that could protect against them.

He spent most of his day, other than when he and the mage went to inspect the crystal, going through the nearby woods to collect wood. He had a pretty decent pile built up on the back wall of his side of the cave.

Although he was glad that nothing had happened yet, he couldn't shake the sense of foreboding that this might only be the calm before the storm.

Later that evening, his mage came rushing back into the cave, seemingly in a great hurry, and looking out the mouth of the cave, as if to check if he had been followed.

"What's the matter?" The king asked.

"I saw some shadow lichs on the way back to the

cave. That's a sure sign that the seal won't hold for much longer. He's getting too powerful for it to contain."

Soon after, they heard a resounding crack and a shattering noise.

The mage went almost white.

"That's it. I think the seal has broken."

They had little time to adjust to this, though, as almost immediately, they had rushed to the mouth of the cave and saw many red, glowing eyes staring in their direction.

A form larger, and it seemed, more solid than the rest could just barely be made out in the dark. It too was heading their way.

"Well, well," came a deep and ominous voice, one

that, although they had never heard it, the mage and the king both knew instinctively had to belong to the dark dragon, "I see that I was not mistaken. Only just broken out of my seal and the descendant of my enemy is already here. I thought I smelled someone of his bloodline. What luck! Bring him to me!"

The order was barely out of his mouth when a horde of shadow lichs was heading for them at amazing speed. The king had a sword and torch of fire in his hand before he knew it, and the mage was bracing with defensive spells and preparing some offensive ones.

The king hacked at the beasts, but that did little damage. He began to flail the torch about to drive them back, although they were still ringing them around. When the king and the mage tried to pause as they got tired, the shadow lichs would lunge again.

Although the struggle seemed doomed, the mage continued casting his spells and the king continued defending against the shadow lichs, all the while, Laubadar was licking his chops, impatient to have them in his clutches.

Despite the fire's efficiency against the dragon-lichs, the mage and the king were eventually worn down. They were knocked out, having been thrown against the wall by a shadow-lich in their exhaustion.

At last, thought the dark dragon, *I have the descendant of my enemy in my grasp.*

However, it was not so, for as he approached, it seemed that a magical force field prevented him from approaching any further.

He looked, and around their necks were the same collars that he remembered the soldiers wearing, that prevented him from harming them, or using his magic against them.

He thought, and soon settled on an idea. His dark aura appeared around the force field, and moved it and the two unconscious dragons within. The force field within his aura levitated and stayed floating in the air; following his motions.

"I might not be able to harm you, or use my magic directly against you, but neither can you fully escape me. I can hold you in my dungeons for as long as need be."

He turned to his shadow lichs, and gave his orders.

"Follow me. I need to check on my lair anyway."

CHAPTER FOUR

Two Months Later...

The sun was already well above the horizon, and getting higher in the sky on the day after the eventful decisions of the council meeting. Those who were destined to be actors in the mission that had been planned were long ago up, and all were feverishly readying themselves in any way they could for the trials ahead. All of them could not forget the importance of the quest they would be going on, and tried to get every little detail right, so as to leave nothing to chance.

The princess was awake early this morning. After the day she'd had yesterday, and the council meeting, she hadn't really slept that well, anyway. She was now packing, as the Council Leader had instructed her, filling her rucksack with things she felt would be useful for the journey. She had taken off all of her jewelry, well almost. She kept her necklace with the royal crest on. Other than that, she knew adornments would either be in the way, or give her away. She remembered this was supposed to be an undercover mission. She did, however, pack things such as a cloak for warmth and possible disguise, and the book, as well as her father's notes. She did not forget the pouch of coins that she had been given for funding the mission. Last, she packed her bedroll and then looked around to see if she had missed anything.

Her companions for the mission were all doing

more or less the same. Targarma was busily selecting magical tomes and bottles of potions that she felt would be most useful. She carefully tucked the pouch full of healing herbs and potions in her rucksack, as well. The last thing she got was her magic staff, which was embedded with jewels which stored and released magical energy.

Across town, in his apartment above the printer's shop where he was apprentice, the scholar Rordgur was packing as well. He chose a few volumes that would help with identifying and translating of writings that they might come across. He grabbed his walking staff for a weapon, and was off.

Elsewhere, Eordwar and Horzkar were also getting ready as best as they could. Horzkar was shining and checking his dragon armor, and choosing his best sword to strap at his side. Eordwar was intently choosing a smaller, concealable weapon, as well as deciding what he could take to allow him to use his talents for disguise and, if necessary, for covert operations. He finally chose a medium size dagger, and strapped it on his belt.

When all were done, they all began to head toward the Council House for one last meeting with the Council Leader.

They were announced and let into the Council Leader's office.

"I have had these brought to me, so that I may give them to you before you set off."

The princess followed his gaze, and her eyes came to rest on five silver collars, each perfect to fit around a dragon's neck, even over armor. They each had a jewel, and she noted the colors matched the colors of their scales.

"These were created by the great mage during the battle with Laubadar with the purpose of preventing his using of his dark magic to harm our side. Let us hope that they will do the same for all of you now."

So saying, he took each collar, and placed it around the necks of each of the dragons, each one getting the one with the jewel that matched their scales.

"They are designed to work with each dragon's magic, while at the same time preventing any outside influences. Also remember, if they detect any such influences, they will act of their own accord, there is no need to magically activate them. You will know they are working when the jewel glows."

"We have arranged for a ship to take you all to the seer, but you must go to the seaside port town to get on it. For the sake of stealth, I recommend you fly there."

"Of course. Thank you for your assistance with the arrangements, and I promise, we will find the objects so that the dark dragon can be defeated."

"I have no doubt of that, princess. Good luck."

And so, they strapped their weapons and sacks on their backs, and the princess took the lead in heading them off in the right direction.

Normally, if she'd been flying by herself, she could have gone a bit faster, but the group had to adjust their pace to the slower flyers, which turned out to be the mage and the scholar.

Suddenly, Eordwar spoke up.

"I just thought of something. Has anyone else here ever been on a ship?"

"Why?" responded the dragon knight, "You seasick or something?"

"I don't know; I've never been on a ship before."

"Well, I hear it helps to stay in your cabin."

The rest of the day's flight went smoothly as well, and towards nightfall they landed, on the dragon knight's advice, and made camp. He started the fire, as he was a fire dragon, and the others began setting up the sleeping palettes.

Soon they were all silently sitting around the campfire, eating the rations that they had packed. The first to speak up was the blue dragon scholar.

Rordgur turned to the princess to address her.

"So, Your Highness, tell me about the history of your royal family. I and my family only came to this realm a few short years ago, so I don't know much about the royalty here."

"Well, that's kind of a long story. Some of the other dragon realms have changed dynasties since the days of my ancestor, King Varthulus, but ours has stayed the same."

"Well, what about the more recent history of your family?"

"That's a little easier. My father, as has become tradition, entered into the knighthood for a period of time, as training for leading soldiers when he became king. During a campaign as a knight, he met a duke's daughter, and insisted on having her and no other."

"So, that was your mother."

"No, his first wife, the Crown Princess; my mother

was his second. They did have a child together, though. My half-brother."

"So, what happened to her and your half-brother?"

"She passed away of illness before my father was crowned, and as for my brother...Well, I never knew him, but all accounts seem to agree that he was an avid archer. He had grown nearly to adulthood, and one day, there was an accident; he was hit by another archer's arrow during his archery practice, and, unfortunately, didn't make it. So, then, my father eventually sought a new wife, and when my mother had me, as the only living child, I had to take his place as the heir."

She continued, "As for my mother the queen, she met him at a royal diplomatic function, as she was the princess of the water realm. The marriage started out as a political alliance, but he eventually came to love her as he did his first wife, although he said he never quite got over her. My mother is the regent that's appointed for him whenever he is away, including now."

"I've been the heir for as long as I can remember, but it seems that, even though I've never met him, I'm living in my half-brother's shadow. I am so coddled that I feel...I don't know, like I am just a replacement for him, instead of myself. I feel they are constantly worried about me. That's why I'm glad that they had no choice this time. I've never been able to do anything like this before. And probably won't again, assuming we make it."

The rest of the meal passed by in more silence, and all soon after retired to sleep. The next morning they all broke camp and continued on their way to the sea port.

Later that day, they arrived, landing outside the gates to present themselves to the guards.

The princess had soon enough taken care of getting them in by presenting their papers, which she had been entrusted with.

They walked through the crowds, all of the citizens churning and bustling about, going on about their lives. The princess was glad that they had no need to carry the burdens that those on the quest did.

Before long, they were coming up to the port, indeed like any other port. One could see many sailors and ships, from all parts of the realms, and the most fascinating of all was the fish market. The group could hardly forbear to gawk at the dragons hawking their wares, mostly fish of all kinds and varieties, some of which were sent to customers in one great toss, or chopped into fillets with a deft hand right in front of a customer's eyes.

As soon as they had passed through the other entrance, the princess began to search to find their ship. The colorful flags and bow figures caught her eyes easily as she scanned back and forth among the ships to search for the one they needed. The sailors and passengers embarking and disembarking from the various vessels excitedly chattered away as she passed them.

She had just passed a few more on the way down the pier when she finally spotted it. She told them to wait there while she checked to see if this was the correct ship and when they would be setting sail for the seer's island.

She questioned the captain, eventually seemed

satisfied with what she had learned, and returned to the group after a few minutes of discussion.

"Well, we are scheduled, and this is the correct ship, but it leaves tomorrow. We might as well book a place in town for tonight, and get some food as well."

So the group turned around, heading back towards the old, brick buildings located nearby the port and its piers; this was the area which held the town's inns.

They found one, a three story with a sign that had a sword and a mace crossed over each other, and got rooms for the night from the innkeeper.

Later, as they sat eating their meal, the topic turned to how to convince the seer to help them.

"Did your father's notes contain any clues as to how he did that?"

"No, unfortunately, and neither did his letter."

"I found out through my studies," said Rordgur "that sometimes seers like to test those who seek their services."

"Like how?" asked the red dragon knight.

"That's what I'm not sure of. They seem to want to know what kind of person they are giving the information to...almost as if they are trying to prevent it from falling into the wrong hands."

They would simply have to deal with that issue as it came up. They would be sailing first thing in the morning, and would be there sometime tomorrow.

Meanwhile, far away, in whipping winds of the high, craggy, and almost sheer mountains of the fire dragon's realms, where the skies above were almost perpetually overcast, there were others at work planning as well. If one looked closely enough, there were signs that an old and long neglected lair was once again being used. Laubadar had returned to his fortress high in the mountain, and was once again setting in motion the plot that had been delayed so long ago.

It was the great, malice-filled black dragon himself, with his four twisted horns and spiked tail, symbols of his corrupting black magic, who sat on the throne there, occupying it again after so many centuries.

His great tail swished in frustration and anticipation in equal measure.

They had then, and still had now, no idea what his true intentions had been back then, he thought to himself. He would not have even bothered to try to conquer the realm of Rhodran if it had not been absolutely necessary to his plans. They made it so. If the other realms' kings had not fended off his dragon-lich armies and fled to Rhodran, he would never have had to follow.

For you see, his plan had been rather larger in scope. Being a master of magics, albeit dark ones, he had learned many secrets that lesser dragon mages were not privy to. He aimed to use his armies to capture the realm's leaders because he was intending to use them to unlock something even more powerful.

The results of his studies seemed to indicate that if one were to magically transfer the powers from one of each type of dragon, and contain them, that would unlock the ultimate power, and allow him to continue his plans, but he hadn't even gotten that far.

However, he was too smart to make the same

mistake twice, and he had fallen to the royal mage the last time. He knew that they would know, if not already, soon enough, throughout the realms that he had returned. They would send someone for the objects the royal mage had created, and they would once again have the power to stop him.

He had made pretty short work, with the help of the dragon-lich army, which he was expanding as he went, to reclaim the ice realm. He was in the process of this in the fire realm, although the king was holding out against him longer than expected.

He did, however, have both the ice realm's king and the king of Rhodran as his prisoners. Normally, he would have already gotten what he needed to know from them and added them to his army of servants, but the mage that had been with Valwardus had cast spells and given a collar to the others and himself to prevent

Laubadar from using his more powerful spells, such as that one, on them.

If he could only figure out how to get past that, but his old foe, the royal mage, was very crafty, especially with these types of things. He had layered the magic so much, that even an adept mage of the dark arts had trouble unraveling it.

At the same time, in the dungeons, Valwardus was himself pondering the situation. He had kept marks on the wall of his cell, keeping time by watching the hours of light and dark out the bars of the window since he had been here, and with the days that they had been on the journey before he had been captured, he reckoned that about two months had gone by.

He could only hope that they had by now set in motion the mission he had given them when he left. He could gather no news of what was happening outside, though, and it could be just as likely that they may be embroiled in defending the realm by now.

From the whispers he heard from the servants and guards, he seemed to gather that they were at a stalemate here in the fire kingdom, though. He was surprised at first that Laubadar had any other followers than his brainwashed undead army, but there were apparently some who were still willing to do so.

Nor had he simply been sitting idly by, counting the days as they passed. His captors had been foolhardy enough to place him in the cell beside his mage, and they communicated back and forth through tapping codes on the walls. It seemed that, as his captors simply had guards posted on the inside and outside of the doors at either end of the dungeon's hallway, they were not aware, or else they simply did not understand the code, which was what the king was hoping for.

He had learned this through his mage, and he had also learned that in the cell beyond his mage's, that they had placed the ice realm's king as well.

He realized that it was just about time for the guard to come in with their food. He had been learning the schedule as well. He was not disappointed, either, for soon he heard the jingling of keys in the lock. The guard quickly put the tray of food on the small stool just a little ways inside the door, and just as quickly left again.

Valwardus was not sure, at least not yet, what he could do with this knowledge, but he knew that it could prove to be a great aid to his escape, given a little more time to think how to use it. He bent down to the stool and picked up his tray to eat. Oh, well, one can never think on an empty stomach, anyway.

Aside from the stool, the only other things that were in the room were a large, wide bench to be used as a bed, and the shackles hanging on the wall. The guards didn't seem to put anyone in those unless they suspected you of making trouble, and the king had so far carefully avoided any appearance of that. They did however, have shackles around his ankles, and attached to that a heavy iron ball to keep him from going anywhere.

His hands were free, at least for now, though, and as soon as the guard had left from clearing away his tray, and he heard the hall door close, he began to converse through the code with his mage again.

He tapped three times, and waited for the signal back. When he heard it, he started their conversation in code.

"Have you heard or learned anything else today?"

"No," came the reply, *"but the ice dragon king says that he heard the guards talking that the fire realm's king is holding out so long because he had received our notice and called for reinforcements before Laubadar's forces arrived. They don't seem to have a clue how the fire realm was so prepared and aware of them coming. I don't think they've figured it out yet, either."*

"Good. Let's hope it stays that way. I'm glad our notifying the others is doing some good," the king tapped back.

"Indeed. Like you, I'm starting to learn the routine of what they do. I don't think it will do us any good, though, until we have some other distraction to attract their attention away from here. Otherwise, they would

be on to us too quickly for us to make an effective escape, and then they would be sure to watch us more closely after that."

"I think you are likely right." the response came. *"All we can do is to wait and see what we can do when some opportune event occurs. Until then, we need to try to find out as much as we can about their plans, immediate and future."*

The king then closed the conversation and went back to his reverie, going over to sit down on the hard, flat bed. How he wished he knew that his family was safe! He couldn't be sure, but he hoped that the fact that the dark dragon was bogged down here in this realm meant he wasn't yet turning his attention to the others.

He snapped his head to attention as he heard the

guards' armor clanking outside, but they didn't stop at his door, and simply kept going.

He picked up the iron ball that was attached to his shackles to move as quickly as he could to the door. He was sure that, in the cell next to him, his mage was doing the same. Through the door's small barred window, and in the dim torchlight that the guards were carrying, he could make out a small group of prisoners that the guards were bringing in.

They were ice dragons, probably one of the last pockets of resistance in the ice realm. They shut one of them in the cell next to him. He could hear the door close.

The king waited until he heard the noise of the clattering in the hallway die down. He then tapped three times on the wall to see if the captive would talk.

He wasn't sure if the other captive could understand code, but it was worth a try.

The captive did respond, and after explaining who he was, the king asked the captive if he had any news from the ice kingdom.

The captive responded that they had been holding out in pockets, especially in the capital, when Laubadar had first returned, although for the most part, the dark dragon did have pretty much control over that realm. He wasn't devoting too much attention to the remainder of the resistance there, though.

The conversation ended without adding much more knowledge than that, but soon there came something that would.

Not long after, he heard a scratching at the bars of the window. He was amazed that anything would be there, after all, it was a window out onto a sheer drop. When he looked, though, he saw a bird, a large hawk that he knew belonged to the fire realm's king. It seemed to have something tied around its leg. It must have snuck in under cover of darkness. He quickly and quietly moved his bench bed over to the window, and untied the paper from around its leg. As soon as he did, the hawk took off back through the darkness.

After quickly moving his bed back, he sat down to read his letter in the dim torchlight of the cell.

"My Fellow Kings,"

"Although we have been holding out so far, the lichs that the dark dragon has created, both shadow and dragon-lichs, seem to keep coming. If we can find a way to break through the ranks, we could get closer to Laubadar's citadel, and perhaps turn the tables on him.

If we are able to do so, take any chance you can to escape behind our lines, and we'll make sure that you don't have to worry about being captured again.

I've also heard tell of some movements in Rhodran. I don't have concrete reports, but it seems to be a small band that has left, although none know for what reason, some suspect that they might have something to do with this whole situation, or rather, how to correct it. Much more than that, I cannot glean from the reports.

I probably won't be able to get another letter to you, so for now, lie low and wait until we can besiege the citadel. Until such time, stay as safe as you can. I hope to be able to free you all soon, and stop the dark dragon in his tracks."

He finished reading the letter, and quickly burned it with the fire from the torch. He couldn't risk them finding that on him. He turned to the walls and passed the information on in code to the others. The responses came back and all agreed to watch and wait for an opportunity that this might present to them.

When he finally had time to ponder the message for himself, he found that he was both proud and terrified. He was proud that his plan was being implemented, and that his daughter had so strongly thrown herself into it, despite the risks, and yet, it was these very risks that terrified him for her sake.

He felt very grateful that he had insisted, despite her mother's protests, that his daughter be taught to use a weapon for self-defense. The queen would allow her nothing more than a dagger.

He almost chuckled as he remembered how her instructor said she had outdone many of the boys after only a few weeks time. He knew that she was more than capable of defending herself, but against this threat?

Well, he thought, *I prepared her as best I could.*

He had to help from this end as best as he could, and that meant being ready to take advantage when the fire realm king made his move.

He put his cloak down across his bed, to make it a little softer, and stretched himself out on the board. No use to think too much about it for right now, and hopefully soon enough between the fire realm's king and the mission he had sent his daughter on, this would be resolved. One way or another.

He focused his eyes on the flames of the torch, and he didn't even realize it when he finally fell asleep.

CHAPTER FIVE

Early on the next morning, the ships on the dock were already pulling out of port, with very few even taking note as the large ships put out on the waters. The small group had awoken early to hurriedly eat their breakfast and rush to the docks. They passed through the crowds yet again, which were large for it being so early, and found their way to the ship they had seen yesterday.

As the group approached, they could tell that the ship, although not one of the absolute newest in the port, was still a mighty ship, and took time to take in its beautiful colors. The keel and the banisters around the decks were painted in vibrant hues, as was the bow figure, which showed a sea serpent in deep greens and blues.

The rest of the ship was not painted, but made of sturdy wood, and the sails were set for leaving port. They could hear the shouts of the crew as they made everything ready for the voyage. On the bow of the ship, just before the anchor port, they could see the ship's name: *The Sea Drake*.

Like any merchant ship, it carried a few cannon for defense purposes, but no more weapons than that, and the crew was not armed.

The captain had let them board the ship, and they began settling in. Before sailing, the captain took time to show them all to their cabin below deck. They all had to share the passenger's room, as the rest of the ship was the crew's large cabin, and cargo storage areas.

There were hammocks hanging, and there were enough to allow them to place their belongings in one and sleep on another.

The group's luggage, such as it was, was soon stowed in the hammocks, and gently swinging with the motion of the ship on the waves. The princess helped to set up five of the hammocks with covers and pillows, and as they were the only passengers for this trip, they had the place to themselves. The captain had been paid very well for their fares, and he took on a little extra cargo to make up for less passengers.

As the group had been informed that the voyage to the seer's island would probably take a few days, sooner with the weather cooperating, they found other ways to entertain themselves while onboard.

The princess, later that day after the sun went down, went up on deck to observe the sea and the stars. She leaned on the railings and looked up to see the many twinkling lights above, which were perfectly reflected in the almost glassy water below. There was no moon out to shine its glare on the water, but that allowed her to see the stars all the better.

She called up to the crow's nest: "Do you see anything out there?"

"No, Your Highness," came the reply, "nothing except sea and sky as far as the eye can see."

Nothing seemed to disturb the scene except for the occasional sound of the lapping of the waves on the side of the ship, or the flap of a sail as it caught a breeze.

Horzkar and Eordwar had spent the day on deck, observing the crew as they went about their tasks, and liked to watch them as they moved deftly about in the sail's rigging, and in the crow's nest.

The scholar and the mage had spent the day below deck in the cabin, studying as much as they could.

The princess took one last look around and looked up at the crow's nest. Perhaps tomorrow she would ask if she could climb up there. She settled down in her hammock once she got back to the cabin, and listened once again to the lapping of the water on the sides of the ship.

The following day, she spent most of her time in the captain's cabin, by his invitation, where he showed her the charts and maps of their route to the island.

"You see this little island here, just off the coast of this big one?" the captain asked as he laid out a map on his desk. "That's your destination. We usually don't go there, but we have sometimes dropped dragons off there before, on special charter, like your group. Our usual destination is here, bringing cargo to the port of the water realm. That's actually going to be our first stop before we drop you off, and then back to port at Rhodran with you once you're done, unless that changes."

"Do you know anything about the seer?" asked the princess, in hopes of getting some scrap of information on her.

"Well," came the reply, "All I know is she's secretive, and most of those who I take to see her don't talk much about her, or their meetings. I wouldn't worry too much about her, though, as I can't remember a time when I brought someone here and they didn't get a meeting with her and get something out of it, even if it wasn't exactly what they were expecting."

The next morning dawned pretty clear, and for most of the day, remained that way. The captain, being an old hand at the sea, said that he could tell that there would likely be rougher weather by the afternoon, though.

Indeed, as the day wore on, the sky grew grayer and grayer, and by late afternoon, it had started a misting rain, which turned into downpours.

This continued intermittently through the night, and by the next day the rain had intensified. The winds had picked up, and were growing stronger. The captain ordered the sails to be furled up, to prevent them from catching and tearing in the wind, and the group was asked to stay below deck.

They could hear the hurriedly shouted orders of the crew above. Only occasionally were these interrupted by the howling of the wind, or the crack of lightning and peal of thunder. The ship was now being tipped back and forth by the waves fairly strongly, and the crew were trying to keep the bow pointed the right direction to keep the ship from being swamped.

"Do you think the ship will be alright?" the princess asked the scholar when they all were essentially stuck below in their cabin.

"I think so. These ships' captains and crews know their stuff, and I'm sure they're doing everything they can to get the ship safely through the storm. They certainly won't rest until they try every last possible effort to prevent any mishaps."

"Let's hope you're right about that." commented the red dragon knight.

Through the next few hours, though the going was rough, and Eordwar nearly becoming seasick with the choppy motion of the waves, the crew managed to keep the boat going in the right direction and keep the waves from overcoming it or rolling it over. Soon enough, the rocking of the ship calmed considerably, and not long after, the captain came down to their cabin.

"We seem to have passed the worst of the storm. It's still raining, and I still suggest you stay below, but we should be able to continue on and reach the port of the water kingdom soon."

The waters calmed enough for the ship to put full sail again, and from then on, they made good time to the first stop, the water kingdom's port.

The call from the crow's nest soon came that land had been spotted, the water realm island could be seen! The ship slid smoothly into port and was tied up and anchored down in no time at all.

Since the group had nothing better to do while they were there, they offered to assist in the unloading of the cargo. The knight and the other male dragons tried to show off by carrying several boxes at once, but the females, the princess and the mage, carried an impressive amount on their own.

The boxes were to be carried all the way down the pier and to a warehouse that stood a little ways down the docks. The purchaser was waiting there at the door to let them in, and while they were going back and forth from the ship, he would count and inventory what they had brought. He seemed to be a fairly prosperous merchant, not uncommon in the water realm.

The process of unloading still took a few hours, and they were still several hours away from the next high tide. Until then, the crew was going to be loading more cargo, bound from the water realm to the other kingdoms, both necessities and luxury goods.

"As soon as we can get out of here on the high tide," the captain assured them, "it won't be long at all until we can get you to your destination. You'll be there before you know it."

In the meantime, they decided to wander the nearby market, which showcased all the goods that came to the realm from all the others. Unlike the port market in Rhodran, which mainly had seafood and other related things, this one had more goods, such as fabrics and furniture pieces. The stalls and stores were stocked with almost anything you could imagine, and some you couldn't: everything from fish and vegetables to books and carpets, even cloaks and a shop selling magic wares.

"Don't they mostly export water here? How do they get all these things?" asked Targarma.

"Yes, they do export a lot of water, as they can use all the water around them in the sea to make fresh water, by way of their powers. This makes Paledat very important to the other realms, and in particular the ice realm. They like having plenty of water, as it makes it easier to use their powers."

"Come to think of it," she mused, "the fire realm gets a lot of its water from here, too. They don't live in a desert, but much of their land is arid mountains. Anyway, although they export a lot of water, as you can see, they also trade a lot for it. It's way more than they need for their kingdom, and some of that excess goes back out as trade with the other realms."

"I didn't know you were so interested in the inner workings of all the other realms." commented the scholar.

"Well, as the heir to the throne, they teach you this kind of thing, so you will be able to carry on diplomacy with the other realms when you inherit the throne."

The male dragons became preoccupied shortly after with a weapons shop, and wanted to stay to check out the stock. The female dragons decided they would continue on through the market.

"Just don't forget to meet us back at the ship, then."

"Don't worry, we'll be there." the princess assured them.

Soon after, a cloaked figure started trailing them, further behind so as to observe them, unnoticed.

The two females were enjoying seeing the wares on offer, and taking an occasional sample of the foods on display, when the princess suggested something.

"I think we have enough time to eat, and it's almost sundown. How about we stop at that tavern over there?"

They entered the brick building, and their pursuer did, as well. They ordered, and when they were done, decided it was time to make their way back down to the docks before the ship left them behind.

It was then that the green dragon mage noticed that someone had been keeping tabs on them.

"Don't look, princess, but I think we're being

followed."

"Followed? You don't think it could be...?"

"It very well could be, but I think we can lose them. Follow my lead."

She picked up her pace, which was matched by the princess, and quickly made a turn down a side alleyway, and then another, following the general direction that they would need to go to get to the docks again.

Like almost anyone inside a labyrinth, though, she took a turn and wound up in a dead end alley. She had gotten lost inside the twisting, turning paths.

They turned around to go back, but saw that their pursuer had already arrived. The princess clutched at her hidden dagger, and the mage's hands and staff began to build up energy.

"Hey, easy ladies. I'm not the enemy." the male red dragon's voice spoke out as he pulled back his hood, which also showed a flash of his guard armor.

"If that's so, then who are you, then?" both female dragons demanded of him at once.

"Right to the point. Good. I'm here because I'm a member of this realm's guards and secret intelligence outfit. We have reason to believe that we have some news that you need to know."

"But why were you following us?" asked the princess.

"To keep an eye on you, to make sure that you didn't have enemies potentially spying on you, and to find a discrete time to brief you. My job is to ensure that your group is safe while you are here."

"Now," the guard explained, "follow me and I'll lead you to the guard station, where I'll debrief you. You might want to put these on, though."

He handed them some cloaks that appeared to be of the style of the water realm.

"These will help you blend in more. If I could tail you, then others could, too. I suggest in the future that you also try to blend in with the locals as much as possible if you have to travel to any of the other realms."

They quickly put the cloaks around themselves and followed him. He lead them back through the maze of alleyways, and they made good time to the guard station. He led them to his office.

"Please, sit down."

"So, why exactly are we here?"

"As I said, for a briefing. We, and all the other kingdoms, had received the message from your father, princess, that the great dark dragon was soon to return, or probably has by now. This was the last we received from him."

"However," he paused, the two female dragons focusing intently, "we then received more news while you were on your journey here. It would seem that the fire king is in the midst of fending off the dragon-lichs, and Laubadar himself."

"What? So he has returned? It's certain?" the mage gasped.

"Apparently so," the water realm guard responded, "and this realm's king, recognizing that your group might be the best hope of beating him, asked me to keep an eye on you and see if you had any others on your trail."

"Do you think the dark dragon knows of our mission?"

"No, princess, at least not yet. Or at least, we have no solid reason to believe that he does. If you are careful, although it will take some doing, you might be able to sneak by under his nose. As I said, you'll have to be very careful at blending in wherever you go."

"There is one more thing that we learned that I think you should know. While it appears that the fire realm is resisting Laubadar's attempts to subjugate it, Machdur has fallen, except for a few pockets of resistance, and Laubadar apparently first returned in the ice realm. Your father was there at the time researching the hiding place of the crystal. The fire king has every reason to believe that he has been captured, along with the ice realm's king."

"Does he know anything more?"

"No, unfortunately, no more than that, at least not in the last message we received. Oh, before you go, I want to give you these, for the other members of your party."

He handed them a rucksack, and when the princess opened it, she saw it contained three more cloaks similar to theirs.

"Thank you. We'd better get going back to the docks, or we're going to miss our ship."

Meanwhile, back at the docks, the loading of the cargo had finished and the two male dragons had returned. They waited on the dock by the ship so they could see the others as they came.

Rordgur was returning from his own excursion into the market, with what appeared to be more books, as well as some food.

"Hey there, bookworm," said the dragon knight, "have you seen the princess and the mage?"

"No, but weren't they with you?"

"They were, until earlier, and they decided to go off on their own. We're waiting for them to come back. I think the crew is almost finished loading, and the next high tide will start soon."

"Are you sure that was the wisest idea? After all, none of us knows this place that well, they could have gotten lost." responded the scholar.

"I don't think they did, but should we go and look

for them?"

"No, that would probably only get us lost and they might come back here in the meantime. It's best to stay right here and wait for them. If they are lost, I think they can find someone to guide them back here."

They were interrupted by the captain coming down the boarding ramp.

"Hello, all. Is everyone here? The cargo's secured in the hold, and it's only about a half hour until the tide."

"We're waiting for the others of our group. We're not sure where they are now, or when they are coming."

"Well, they'd better hurry. If they don't come soon, we'll miss the tide. We won't go without you, but the next tide won't be until tomorrow morning." With that, the captain turned and walked back up the gangplank.

"So," said the dragon knight to the scholar, pointing at his bundle that he had under his arm, "what did you decide to buy?"

"Oh, some books from the bookstore. They're all about languages. Since I was chosen as a sort of interpreter for this mission, I figured it would help to give myself a refresher course, and add some to my knowledge while I was at it. Sorry I took so long, by the way. I always tend to get lost in a bookstore, I never seem to know when to stop, and what exactly to buy versus what to put aside. I have a hard time deciding among so many good books."

"I figured as much," chuckled the red dragon, "don't worry about it though, me and Eordwar are about the same when it comes to weaponry. We wanted to stay in the weapons shop, but the others wanted to go on, that's why we got separated in the first place. I wound up buying a new sword and a good strong mace. Never know when you'll need one of those in battle. Wait a minute though, can you tell if that's them coming?"

He pointed to two cloaked figures following behind a third, who seemed to be directing them towards the docks. They were all coming down the hill from the marketplace, and seemed to be fairly easily making their way through the thick crowds. Eordwar had now joined the other male dragons on the pier, coming back off the ship, and he caught up with them as they waited for the figures to approach.

The evening twilight was coming on as the two dragonesses of the little band followed the cloaked figure ahead of them that was making its way as quickly as possible through the marketplace, and on towards the docks.

"I can see the docks. We'll be there soon." the mage said to her traveling companion, who nodded in response.

The figure they had been following stopped and let them pass at the end of the pier.

"Thank you for your help." the princess said to the guard, who nodded and turned to start back to the guard house.

They continued up the pier and before long heard the shouts of the rest of their group.

"So," teased Eordwar "who was Mr. Mysterious we saw leading you here? You get lost and have to have someone show you the way?"

"You could say that." said the mage.

"We'll have to tell you all about it when we get on the ship." the princess added.

Almost as if on cue, the captain called "Oh, good, you're all here, now. Hurry and get on board, the tide is starting and we have to put out before it goes out again."

They all trundled on board, the gangplank was removed, the sails were set, and the anchor weighed, all with expert precision and timing.

The water and wind soon had them pulling out of the port, and not much longer after that, the port was small on the horizon.

The captain informed them that the journey to the island would be completed by daybreak.

"Really, that quickly?" asked the scholar.

"Yeah, I told you it wasn't far."

They made their way down to the cabin and then, as promised, the princess told them what they had been told by the guard.

"Personally," remarked Horzkar, "I think you were pretty lucky that it wasn't an agent of Laubadar. It easily could have been. I've got to say I'm relieved that they don't believe he knows, though. I wonder how long we can keep it that way, but we've got to do our best to make sure to lie low for as long as we can."

Asvartha said that from now on, they would have to be careful if they split up while they were still traveling, and that they should be on alert at all times, now that they were aware there was a chance that Laubadar was onto them and might be searching for them.

The others agreed. The princess gave the cloaks to the other three of the group that had not been with them.

"You know, I think I need to do more research on cloaking and invisibility spells," said the mage. "There's no need to hold anything back that might help us."

So saying, she dived into reading her spell books, and they could tell that it would be a while until she was done.

She continued her studies, as they were careful not to interrupt her, and for the most part spent the remaining time until they reached the island in finding things to do in other parts of the ship. She found some powerful offensive spells as well as the ones she was searching for, and began to practice all of them to get them absolutely right. She would need firepower as well as defense, and she had to make sure that she could perform the spells flawlessly; there would be no room for error in the midst of a battle.

The scholar, meanwhile, took to studying his new books that he had bought at the market. He loved learning new languages, and if it also provided a useful skill that would enable them to complete the mission, all the better. He also made sure to refresh himself on those he knew already.

When the others returned to the cabin, it was late, and they all retired to bed. It seemed like they hadn't slept very long, though, when they were awakened by the sounds of the shouts of the crew, and the anchor being dropped.

"I think we must have arrived," the scholar told the

others, "because they don't drop anchor like that unless they've reached their destination. Someone will probably be coming soon to tell us to get up to the decks, so we might as well be ready."

They quickly got themselves ready, and just as the scholar had expected, while they were doing so they still heard occasional shouts that they knew were crewman making things ready for their excursion to shore. The princess hoped it would be light enough by the time they got up to the deck to get a view of the island. She had to admit she was kind of curious to see what an island inhabited only by a seer would look like.

<u>CHAPTER SIX</u>

As the captain had promised, they had arrived near the island not long before daybreak. The captain came to inform them just before sunrise.

"Alright, we've anchored just offshore of the seer's island." he told them. "I'll have my crew take you out there in the dinghy. There is no port here, or at least large enough for a ship this size, so that's the only way to go ashore."

They all filed out of the cabin and up to the decks,

and got their first sight of the island. It was a relatively small island, especially when compared to the size of the water realm's island. It didn't seem to be more than a few dozen acres, and had a ring of beach around it. They could just make out in the growing light a small pier. It was just as the captain had said, there was no way a large ship could get near there.

They could see the captain further down the deck, barking orders for the dinghy to be lowered to the water, and tossing the rope ladder down to the two crew in the boat below. They caught the bottom of the ladder, and the captain secured the top to the ship.

"Alright," he announced once they were finished, "It's ready for you. I have to tell you though, if all of you are going, it might take a couple of trips. The dinghy can only hold two or three others besides the crew."

"All right, we need to make a decision. We need to know if we're all going, or some will go and some will stay. Do all of you want to go? Would anyone prefer to stay here?" The princess asked the group.

"I really should stay and keep practicing my cloaking spells." Targarma said sheepishly.

"And I have never really been interested in fortune tellers," chimed in Eordwar.

"Well I'll go. I shouldn't have let you go alone before, and it is my duty to make sure you're protected." answered Horzkar.

"I'll go as well," said Rordgur, "I've never met a seer before, and I think it would be a good subject to learn about, from a scholar's point of view, of course."

The three who had decided to go climbed down

the rope ladder and carefully entered the small dinghy. The two crew members had rowed them to the pier, and tied up the dinghy in short order.

"We'll wait for you here," one of them said. "Do what you need to, and when you're done, we'll take you back."

The princess thanked them, and looked around for some sign of where the seer's house or cave would be. It would almost seem that the island was deserted, if they didn't know better.

More than likely to keep out any unwanted visitors, she thought to herself.

There was nearby what seemed to be somewhat of a path through the trees and undergrowth, though, and likely that was the only way in.

"Come on," she called to the others, "that must be it. Let's go."

The now smaller group crossed the beach, and headed up the narrow way, now shaded by all the trees making a canopy.

Although the path was somewhat clear, it was certainly not kept up, some parts had shrubs and undergrowth coming over the trail, which the dragon knight cleared with his sword.

"I wonder what those tests were that they said the seer likes to put to those who come here?" the blue dragon mused.

They all got the answer soon enough. They had not yet gone very far up the trail, when they came to the first fork, and had to choose which direction to go.

"Do you suppose this is like a maze? To test one's wits?" the princess asked the scholar.

"Well, I don't know if there are any more forks in the path, but if there are, it very well could be. Perhaps the challenge is to get to the seer in the first place."

"Well, how do we know which path to choose?" asked the dragon knight. "If we choose the wrong one, we could be wandering around all day."

"There's really no way to tell unless you have either a map or a bird's eye view of the island, and with this thick canopy above us, I think trying to fly up to see things is not going to work. I also somehow doubt that the seer would be handing out maps."

"So we just have to pick and hope we get it right?" the princess mused.

"Yes, for this one and any others we might come across."

The princess sighed, and thought a moment. When she had made her decision, she came to attention and started off. "Come on, let's go this way. Might as well get it over with. We can't just stand here all day debating, either."

They noticed that the path had turned to the left when they had entered it from the beach, so they kept to the trails that lead in that same direction, in the hope that it would lead them around the outside of the island. There was no way to tell if this was the correct solution, or if their destination was on the interior of the island.

There were no directions or trail arrows of any sort, and many times it seemed the trail just petered out, but they managed to clear away the trail and keep going forward. The princess began to notice that it seemed the trail was indeed circling the island, but was curving ever more sharply inward, towards the denser areas in the center.

Finally, after what seemed like an eternity of wandering up and down the trails of the island, they found a path that seemed to go towards the middle of the island, and when they took it, they spotted the end of their search, the reason they came: the home of the seer.

And it was none too soon, either, because although the canopy naturally blocked out a lot of the light that otherwise would have reached them, they could tell that it was late afternoon, and they weren't sure if they wanted to be out in the open once darkness fell.

As they approached, they could tell it was a small hut, and barely looked large enough to hold all of them inside it. It was made of large, thick logs for the walls and roof, and had many years of moss growth covering it, not to mention shrubbery and undergrowth surrounding it. Hanging from the corner of the eaves nearest the door, there was a lantern, and it was already lit.

A great tree, probably one of the oldest on this entire island, stood behind it, and indeed might have been used to make up part of one side of the back of the hut.

The princess was the first to approach, and gave a knock at the door.

The three heard a voice from within: "Come in, I've been expecting you."

They entered, making sure to close the creaking wooden door behind them, and were surprised at how the seer was able to make such a small place so relatively inviting and cozy. There was plenty of furniture, and carpets and rugs to cover the floor. The house was not divided into any rooms, as it was too small for that, but one could tell that the house was still absolutely livable and functional in every necessary way.

As the princess looked around, she noticed that there was actually a little open doorway, seeming to lead into a nook that had been carved into a hollow of the tree, the one seen from outside, that had been used to make up the back right corner of the house. The logs that made up the other sides, and the roof, seemed to be nailed directly into the tree, as one would sometimes see a fence in like manner. There seemed to be no bed furniture out here where they were, so perhaps that's what she used it for. Altogether, it gave a very charming effect to the whole place.

They soon heard a whistle from a kettle that was on the wood-burning stove in the corner, and a voice, followed by its owner, came from the nook.

"Sorry to keep you waiting, would anyone like some tea before we begin?"

They turned to look at the seer, a female blue dragon, wearing an elaborately embroidered cloak with shades of blue and purple, the last of which matched her eyes. It was elegant, yet still of the same style seen in the water realm.

"No, thank you, at least for me." the princess said, with the others following suit.

"Very well. I am called Regartha, the seer and prophetess. Your father the king was here, not long ago, princess."

As she spoke, she set a large, bejeweled, and very ornate bowl, which was full of water, on the table in front of them.

"Actually, I know we're here for the mission, but I was wondering if you could tell me any news about my father. The last I heard was that he had been captured on his mission."

"Yes, he did indeed proceed to his mission, and there was captured, as you say, but unfortunately, due to the dark magical influence around it, I cannot divine the future or present for anyone within Laubadar's citadel; it interferes with my scrying visions."

"Scrying visions?" asked the scholar.

"Yes, that's how I practice my divination, through scrying. You need a smooth, reflective surface, such as a mirror or a bowl of water, like I have here, and you can call visions to appear in the reflective surface."

"How does that work?" he asked, curious for the answer.

"Well, there are no true seers who aren't also mages, so, the answer is, we use our magic to make it happen. There are particular spells which cause this to happen, but the essential answer is it is a magical doctrine that we practice."

"Oh, so you are mages, too?"

"Yes, and this particular branch has been learned by the mages of the water realm for untold centuries. I myself learned it from a master who was the one hundred and seventh in an unbroken line from master to apprentice, and I am his apprentice, having trained my own already as well."

"I had a question, too," inquired the red dragon knight, "What is the maze all about? It took us nearly all day, and that was with a whole lot of luck. Is it some sort of magic maze that misdirects you?"

"No, that's not magic, but I think it's important to make sure that those who come here prove their wits. It could take a long time to find me here, unless one figures out the secret of how to get through it. Also, it doesn't hurt as a deterrent to all of those who might come here with the intention of using the knowledge I give for less than upstanding purposes. I also have to warn you here and now that, while I see a lot, I don't divulge everything that I do see. Bad things usually happen when a seer reveals more of the future of a client than they should."

"Back to your question, though, princess, as far as I can tell from the last vision that I had of him, he was safe at that time, due to wearing the protective collars, like you have. As long as he doesn't ever take it off, Laubadar can't touch him."

"Thank you for telling me what you can."

"That's my job. Now, what you are here for. I will use my divining magic to see what you need to do."

She began to recite and repeat a short incantation over the bowl, moving her hand gently over it. Soon the surface of the water in the bowl began to glow, as did the seer's eyes.

After a few minutes of seeing what the visions told her, she began reciting another spell, and slowly the glow stopped.

"I have seen what you must do. There are instructions left by the royal mage himself in his journal. Do you have it with you?"

The scholar brought out the black, leather bound book and laid it on the table. Meanwhile, she went over to a desk and withdrew a paper.

"This is a page from the journal, it was left to my ancestor by the owner of that journal."

"You must read..." she said, turning the pages to a section near the back, which showed where her page had been torn out, "...this section here. It will tell you what you need to know."

The scholar picked up the book, and began reading the page and the section that the seer had indicated aloud to the others:

"...I knew at once that the key to everything was Laubadar's final curse against the family of the king. I could turn this not only to the good of the royal family, but to Laubadar's unwitting causing of his own destruction. There was the way to ensure that he would never be able to come back and permanently threaten our realms again.

I cast my spells, so that, by Laubadar's own curse, he could come back as long as the royal family existed, but that they themselves would be the only ones able to use the only weapons, my weapons, that were the only thing that could stop him.

I do not know if he will ever attempt this, but if he does, he will simply be in for layer upon layer of obstructions. Another precaution, just like all of the others I have taken.

CHRONICLES OF RHODRAN

The two great magical objects, I have endeavored to hide in one realm, while the prison of the dark dragon is in another. This book, meanwhile, shall remain in its hiding place as an extra measure.

The idea came to me to ensure their safety by creating a map to the location of the magical objects, which would aid the royal family in their quest, should they need to face Laubadar again, and yet, to keep it out of the wrong hands, to split it into four and put each piece in one of the other realms besides Rhodran.

The first piece is in the fire kingdom. The king there knows where it is, however, my protective spells mean there is a special test to reach it, as with all the other pieces of the map. The test of the fire realm is a test of strength, so a knight will be needed to successfully complete it.

The second is in the ice realm. In this case, there is a test which regards knowing what to do by reading the inscriptions of the walls of the chamber. A scholar would be required to pass this test.

The third is in the earth realm. The test for this one is tricky, and requires one to keep one's cool and not be fooled by traps and misdirection while making their way around a field that requires one to dodge, avoid, or overcome obstacles. Having someone with a great deal of cunning is an asset here.

The last is in the water realm, and is just as tricky. It requires a vast knowledge of magic to even enter the test. A strong mage is a necessity to pass this test.

If one is able to gather all four pieces of the map from completing these tests, they will know the final location to go to get the magical gauntlet and spear.

There is also a test to prevent just anyone from getting the objects themselves, and of course I did not neglect to cast protective barriers around the location where I sealed Laubadar's crystal.

The test for the objects is one which only a silver dragon can complete. There is a spell I cast which will sense which type of powers the silver dragon has, and adapt the test to that.

All these preparations I completed while I was away from the kingdom, and I felt once I had done all this, that the kingdom would now be fine on its own. I designed this so that no one dragon could complete the tests on their own, and that only one of the king's bloodline could finish the final test and receive the gauntlet and spear.

Once received, the gauntlet has a tremendous

magic absorption ability that not only protects the wearer, but also weakens the user of dark magic.

Once he is weakened, the user of the gauntlet can also then use the spear. It contains a powerful magic that places my great barrier seal around anything, inanimate or living, that is touched by the tip of the spear while it is activated. It is activated by holding it with the hand covered by the gauntlet.

Both of these objects have protective spells that prevent them from being used by any being who uses dark magic, as a final fail-safe against Laubadar.

All of these fail-safes may seem overmuch, but as someone who has seen firsthand what destruction the dark dragon has wrought, and these weapons being the only chance of stopping him, there is no recourse that must not be tried to prevent him or his followers from *ever getting their claws on these weapons, and so that they will be available to those who need them.*

Any future king who has need of these objects, then, will have to gather a group of the necessary dragons with the necessary skills, and find the map first. If the king is unavailable, then it must be a silver dragon of his bloodline."

As the scholar dragon finished reading and closed the book, the other members of the group took to pondering what this all meant.

"So what we have to do, is go to all the different realms and pass these tests, in order to gain access to the map of where the magic weapons are hidden? Although, since it does say to go to the fire realm first, there may be a way to ask the fire realm's king for advice."

"He won't be able to help you much, it has to be you or one of your group to finish each test at each location," replied the seer, "but, if it's any consolation, I did see that you successfully arrive at the final battle, but I cannot tell you how the final battle with Laubadar goes."

"Well," spoke up the dragon knight, "if what that journal says is true, we should have a fair advantage as long as we have the princess."

"At least we finally have a direction that we've been pointed to go in. We know what to do. Thank you."

"You're most welcome, princess. Now, since I don't even need to look to know it's dark outside by now, you three shall just have to stay here tonight. In the morning, as soon as it's light, you can go back to the ship, and you can then be on your way to your first stop. You wouldn't make it back now, you were skilled enough as it was to be able to find your way here in the daylight."

She conjured some pads for them on the floor. They all settled in, agreeing that stumbling around through the woods around the house in the night would not be the wisest decision.

They slept quite comfortably, considering that they were on pallets on the floors, and since the forest was all around, they awakened to the dappled sunlight filtering in the windows and birdcalls the next morning.

The seer made them some tea, and offered them some breakfast cakes.

"I wonder how we'll find our way back through that maze of forest? We were lucky to get here in the first place," the knight asked the others.

"Don't worry, I'll lead you. There's a shortcut to get back as well, that you wouldn't know coming here."

The group finished their breakfast, and helped the seer dragon to clean up before they left. She showed them the way that was the quickest route back to the beach. Very soon they could see the light coming through the trees at the end of the path.

The seer pointed and said, "There you are. Just follow the path the rest of the way, and you'll be at the beach in no time."

The group saw, as they came onto the beach, a bunch of cargo boxes, and nearby, a temporary tent set up for them. They were just wondering what was going on, when some members of the crew approached them.

"Sorry for the mess, but we were left here to let you know. The ship was inspected on the captain's orders while we were waiting for you, seeing as how we had not had a chance yet since the storm to do so. Some repairs were found to be necessary. We had to remove the cargo to do them, and will need probably until morning tomorrow to complete the repairs that are needed, and get the cargo back on board the ship before we can get back underway. In the meantime, we've moved all of you to the tent there on the beach. Your friends are waiting for you there already. Don't worry, though, our shipwright that's in our crew is one of the best. He'll have the work done, and we'll be back on our way as soon as possible."

They headed towards the tent, where they found the rogue resting and the mage still engrossed in her studies. The princess entered to bring them up to date.

The scholar sat down to jot down some notes for himself on what he'd learned about the seer.

"Say, since everyone else is busy, why don't we practice our skills a little. I know it's not exactly the same type of skills as the others, but we have to keep ourselves sharp, too." the knight suggested to the rogue.

"Sure, why not, I don't have anything else to do."

They chose an empty spot a little further up the beach, and soon the sounds of clashing metal could be heard up and down the beach.

The knight with his sword, and the rogue with his dagger, parried and thrust against each other until they had to take a break. They were both as exhausted as if they had been in a real battle.

"I think that's pretty good for now," remarked the knight, "I just wanted to practice a little, since it seems that I'll be the first one up when it comes to the challenges."

The group rested well that night, with each of them having contemplated the role that they could take in the upcoming challenges and trials, and in the morning, not long after they had awakened, they saw the dinghy coming from the ship, and that the cargo had been stored away again. Some crew members began to take down the tent.

The repairs having been made, and the cargo once again safely in the hold, the crew told them that they could now board the ship, and they would soon make ready to sail. The crew took them back, as before on the dinghy, and they boarded the ship.

The princess had talked with the captain, who wanted to know if they would be going back to Rhodran or whether they had to go somewhere else.

"The seer informed us that we need to go to the fire realm, Teldros, first, and then on to the other realms as well."

"All right, then, I'll chart the course for the fire realm. When we get there, will you need our services further?"

The princess thought a moment. "It's more than likely that we won't, since all the other kingdoms are connected via land. We'll likely be able to find land transport when we need it."

The captain nodded, and began to chart the course. The princess returned to the cabin.

In what seemed no time at all, the ship was off again, amidst the shouts of the crew and the flapping of sails in the wind, heading back north, their next destination, and the real start of their journey.

CHAPTER SEVEN

The journey to the realm of the fire dragons went much more smoothly than had the one to the island of the water realm. The group was almost excited to find themselves pulling into the pier, and getting ready to disembark to start the first test. They knew it would be a test of strength, but they were anxious to see exactly what kind of test it would be, and then to pass it so they could get the map piece and move on to the next trial.

Just as the princess was getting ready to find someone among the crowd at the docks to ask directions to get to the fire king's palace, they saw approaching a group of guards, all with the crest of the fire king on their armor.

After greeting them, the captain of the regiment explained that they had come to escort them to the palace, for their safety, as they had been sent by the king's authority.

"You see," the captain continued, "although we have been holding off Laubadar's forces, and still are, it's a possibility that he might have sent agents to waylay you on your journey. The king is off at the front lines, so we were sent by the king's chancellor to come here."

"Oh, I almost forgot," he added, bringing out a parcel, "here, these are for you, to help you blend in while you're here."

They opened the parcel, and found some garb for each of them in the style of the fire realms. They changed out of their cloaks from the water realm and into the new garments as quickly as they could on the ship and returned to the guards.

"All right," said the captain, "now we head to the palace to see the chancellor. It's a bit of a walk from here, but you'll be alright, I suppose. Stay in the middle of our formation as we go."

The group of five positioned themselves as they were directed, and the march proceeded on.

As the group came up on the palace, carved straight out of the rock of the mountain, just as the rest of the city was, it was easy to see that it could almost rival the palace of Rhodran, at least in size, and probably also in magnificence.

A giant cave had long ago been cleared by the ancestors of these dragons, which ended up almost hollowing out the mountain, and some of the giant rocks on the cave floor had been left to be carved and hollowed out into houses and, most noticeably, the great palace. The port had been made by connecting a canal from the city, out the large mouth of the cave, and into the sea, which filled the area of the cave in front of the city with an artificial lake.

The palace's flags were flying, showing that the process of government was still going on, despite the conflict with Laubadar.

The guards stopped to answer the challenge from the guards at the door, and were allowed to pass. They all entered, and saw almost at once that the chancellor had been waiting for them.

"Ah, good, you're here. Thank you, guards, you may return to your posts now."

The guards did so, with a small salute to the chancellor before they all went their separate ways through the palace back to their regular duties.

"Now, I've got to say I'm glad you're here. I'm in charge of making sure your group is safe while you are all in our realm, in the absence of the king."

"I must say I'm curious as to what the escort was all about." the princess asked, after having made her greetings to the chancellor.

"Well, I don't know how much you've gotten as far as updates, but the battles are going back and forth here in Teldros, and have been for several weeks. We have been holding the line, and haven't seen any shadow lichs, or any other agents of Laubadar here in the city, being this far from the front, but it's best to err on the side of caution, and not risk him trying to intercept and capture you, especially now."

"Of course," he continued, "that leads into why I'm here. I'm to explain to you where and how the trial will proceed, and should you prevail, how to access the location of the map. The trial will be a test of strength, as you might know. Who will be your champion for the trial?"

"I guess that's me," the dragon knight spoke up. "What weapons are we allowed to use?"

"Oh, this is a test with no weapons. It is a tournament, which will test your strength through strategy rather than weaponry. You must wrestle your opponents bare handed and overcome them to win."

"Oh, so it's a wrestling contest, then? I think I can

handle that."

"Good luck to you, champion. Here are the rules. There will be eight competitors, counting you, and there will be three rounds, elimination style. You will have to defeat your opponent in every round to be the winner. No holds which are normally not allowed will be allowed here."

"So then, when does the contest start?"

"First thing tomorrow, at the amphitheater here in the city. We've already chosen the other participants, and don't get too cocky, because they won't be easy."

So saying, the chancellor led them to their rooms for the night. Before he left, he gave them some final advice.

"Champion, I suggest you get your rest tonight, you'll need to conserve your energy for tomorrow. The rest of you might consider that solid advice as well. I'll be back early, to wake you up and lead you to the stadium."

True to his word, he awakened them early to let them know he would be back in half an hour to guide them to the stadium, so they should prepare in the meantime.

The knight got himself dressed in his wrestler's gear: he bound his hands and knuckles, and left all his other gear and armor in the palace.

The chancellor brought them safely to the amphitheater for the contest, and as they saw it, they had to admit that the fire realm knew how to make impressive buildings.

The amphitheater of Teldros, though it did indeed qualify as ancient, was actually one of the most recently built edifices in the whole city. It was the only one that had been built with stone, rather than carved directly out of the rock as the cave that protected the city had been carved out. It stood four stories high, enough to seat thousands of spectators, and the flags of the fire realm, with the official colors, red and orange to represent fire, flew proudly from the top. The stone facades were all carved with scenes depicting great events and contests that had been held there. It was used for all sorts of sports, events, and celebrations, as well as a place of meeting, where necessary.

The chancellor got them in, and showed Horzkar the room where he would wait as a contestant. The other contestants were already there as well, and they could see that some of them looked like brutes. There were a couple of large red dragons, a couple of green ones not much smaller, and three more blue ones. All except the red dragons had come to compete as challengers from other realms than the fire realm. The organizers of the tournament were keeping it all about level, though, because Rhodran's dragon knight was not far behind the other competitors in terms of size and bulk.

The chancellor then showed the rest of the group to the seats. Being as this was for the trials, they were the only spectators, and they sat impatiently awaiting the start of the contest.

The first match was announced, and proceeded. The group was anxious to see their companion's match, but they had to wait through the first three of the first round. The other three matches proceeded, and soon their friend was in the ring.

There were no ropes around the ring, it was all

open, but there were, of course, lines on the floor showing the boundaries of the ring. The opponent had to be pinned to the ground in the ring or it wouldn't count.

Horzkar's first opponent was one of the red dragons that they had seen. Rhodran's champion got in a couple of good grips before the red dragon countered and broke his grip. The dragon knight kept himself alert, and circled, trying to find an opening to use.

The bigger dragon suddenly rushed, but Horzkar, being slightly lighter, managed to dodge.

Eventually the match ended when Horzkar was able to tire his opponent out and pin him to the ground.

The second round matches proceeded, with the Rhodran champion winning his match there as well.

The final match came, and it appeared that the dragon knight was going up against one of the blue dragons. Horzkar dodged and tried to get a grip on the opponent where he needed to, although there were a couple of times he had to break grips from his opponent that almost got him to the ground, and had to roll to avoid being pinned for the count.

He finally managed to get behind and use a grip that caused the blue dragon to fall to his hands and knees, and the Rhodran champion was able to use his weight to pin the opponent to the ground, and win the final match.

The chancellor came up to congratulate him.

"Well, champion, those were some of our strongest, and you still managed to beat them and win. Congratulations, you have won the trial for your group.

It was an excellent win."

"I've got to admit," replied Horzkar, shaking the chancellor's hand, "you were right. That wasn't a walk in the park. I had to dodge and break free a lot more than I usually do. You wouldn't think such big guys could also move that fast. If I had not succeeded in keeping my distance, it would have gone a lot differently."

The chancellor then took them back to the palace, and later that evening feasted them in celebration of their victory.

"Now, to get down to the other business at hand. Now that you have won, you may claim your prize for the trial, which is the way to, and location of, the map piece that the fire realm protects."

"To get there, though," he explained, "is normally a long and arduous journey to the mountains north of here. It resides in the mountain called commonly the Spear's Point. However, there is an alternate route to get there. It is an underground maze of secret passages that the first king here had built, which even Laubadar doesn't know of, as far as we can tell. They allow one to pass underground throughout the whole city and some of the kingdom beyond. It comes out near the bottom of the Spear's Point, and the cave that holds the map piece is nearby, but you will need your mage to release the protective spells to enter and retrieve it."

"So, you're giving us permission to use these underground routes to go to the mountain?"

"Yes, the king said, should you pass the trials, that he granted you permission to use his private secret passageways. Anyway, it's the best way to avoid Laubadar finding out what you are doing. The front lines are not far from where you would be passing by, if you were to use the land route."

So saying, he gave them provisions and supplies for the journey, and called for a lantern. He led them through the palace hallways, with the group barely having time to admire the furniture and artworks to be found there, and all the way to the back rooms of the palace. He stopped in front of a simple wooden door.

"Now, I'm going to light the lantern, because it's going to get dark from here on out. Oh, yes, here," he said, handing two more lanterns to the group, one to the princess and one to the scholar. "One of you should lead and one bring up the rear with these lights. I'll take you down to the chamber, but I can't go the whole way with you."

They followed him through the door, and found themselves in an apparently little used storeroom. He went down the stairs and crossed to the back wall. A secret panel slid aside to reveal the passageway.

The short passageway beyond led to some narrow, spiraling stairs cut into the rock, which went down into a smaller chamber, with several rock passageways leading off of it, that was deep below the surface of the city.

"That middle one on the far wall there, that's the one that leads to the mountain. It will come out in a small cave in the forest just before the mountain. Take the straight path and you'll get there."

So, after thanking the chancellor, who took his leave to go back up to the palace, the small band started down the path he pointed out, in single file, with the princess at the rear, and the scholar at the front.

The narrow rock passageway would never have permitted them to pass any other way. They could occasionally hear the knight's sword scraping the sides of the rock walls, so tight was it in some spots.

The mage had lit a magical flame which she carried in her palms to add to the light. It was a small flicker, like of a candle, but without anything to burn.

Their packs seemed to weigh them down more and more, with no way to tell what time it was above ground, day or night. There was no way to know how long they had been walking, nor how much longer they had to go.

They soon, however, came to a smaller cave chamber, and they could see that the passageway continued, as there was another passageway that opened out from the opposite wall.

The group decided to take a break here, and set down their packs to rest for a while.

"How much further do you think this goes?" asked the mage.

"Not sure, but probably miles. If I had to guess, I'd say we've only been at this for a few hours now. I've been counting our steps, and if the average steps per hour holds true, that's about how long it's been." answered the scholar.

"You know how to keep track of that?" asked the mage, shocked.

"Well, I can't be totally sure that it's accurate, but as close as we're going to get in these narrow, dark tunnels, with no other reference point to use."

As they came down the pathway, they found

several other stopping points, and stopped for a while to rest at least every other one that they came to. According to the scholar, they were random points along the path, as best as he could tell, as they were not evenly spaced from each other. Occasionally they would see another path jutting off of the main one they were on, but they knew not to take those, and kept going straight ahead.

The scholar and the knight took turns being the lead lantern holder, and the group seemed to be making good time until the knight came to a stop.

"What's happened?" called the princess from the rear.

"I think I see the path blocked up ahead. Stay here and let me go a little further up and check it out."

When he returned, he confirmed that the path had

been caved in somehow.

"I guess they must have had a cave-in that they didn't know about. Anyway, we'll have to clear it to go on."

"Here, they gave us these two pickaxes here for just such a thing," said the scholar, handing one to Eordwar. "Let's get started. The sooner we get this finished, the sooner we can get going again."

"I saw another passageway jutting off a little ways back. Maybe the mage and I can carry the rubble to there to get it out of the way as you're clearing the tunnel," the princess volunteered.

"And I've got my mace," said the knight, "I can help to smash those rocks up."

So they all went to their jobs, and after a while, the

tunnel was once again clear for them to move on.

They finally reached the end of the tunnel, and could see the light coming from the entrance of the small cave that the tunnel terminated in.

"Ah, man! Fresh air at last!" said the dragon knight.

"And don't forget light." added the scholar.

The sunlight was shining down through the trees of the forest in dapple patterns. Off to their right, there was a great mountain, and they didn't need a label on a map to tell it must be the Spear's Point.

They put out their lanterns and headed out of the cave's mouth.

It didn't take them long at all to arrive at the base of the mountain. The mage cast a locating spell and soon had discovered the point of entry, where the protective spells were, and had not long after dissipated them to allow entry.

They re-lit their lanterns and made their way cautiously down the short path. It soon opened up into a single small chamber. In the back, there was an alcove where they discovered the first piece of the map.

All along the chamber walls, there were carvings and inscriptions of all sorts. The scholar took some time to read them before they collected the map, in case they contained any other information that might be useful.

"Well, it basically just tells about why this was set up and by whom, so nothing we don't already know," he said after he had finished translating the inscriptions, "but, they date to the right time, so we are definitely in the right place."

It was a sheet of parchment, which had parts of a map on it, and a border along two of the sides.

"Just as the journal says, it must be part of a set, and when you put them together, you get the whole map." the scholar mused.

The princess carefully tucked the page in the journal, and the scholar put his rucksack back on. They proceeded back outside and then to the mouth of the tunnel to make their way back.

They were especially glad when they found themselves nearly at their goal, they came into the chamber that was deep underneath the palace, went back up the spiral staircase, and up through the storeroom and into the palace.

The chancellor was surprised to see them back so soon, and said that they had only been gone for a few days, less than a week. He told them that normally the trek, at least overland, to the Spear's Point usually took more than a week. The scholar was happy to know that that had been close to what he had estimated. The chancellor then invited them to a grand dinner with him that night before they left for their next destination.

"Personally, though, I'm just happy to be back above ground and out of those cramped tunnels. I hope none of our other trials has us doing something like that again." the dragon knight stated, as he sat down to the dinner.

The following morning, the chancellor came to speak with them, as he had promised the night before.

"I suppose you must be on your way soon to the next realm? Have you given thought to what mode of transport you want to use to get there?" he asked, directing his question to the princess.

"I hadn't really thought about the transport, but yes, we do need to go soon."

"Well, I might be able to help with that. Before he left, the king gave me permission to lend you some of our swiftest warhorses, that is, if you're not adverse to riding."

"No, we can ride." the princess replied, "and thank you so much for your generous offer."

"It's no trouble at all, not for the princess of Rhodran and her guards. I'll have them saddled and ready as soon as you say."

"We're pretty much already packed and ready to go, so you can have them start now, if possible."

"As you wish, princess." The chancellor turned to

another servant and gave him the orders to have the grooms saddle and bridle the horses, and bring them to the front court. He then turned back to the five dragons.

"I also wanted to let you know, that as the ice realm is temporarily without a king, due to him being captured, the fire king wanted me to pass on some advice to you: he knows of the location of the leader of the rebellion against Laubadar in the ice realm, and he suggests you go to them to get help finding the location of the test, and perhaps the map. The ice king might have left important news or papers with them that could lead you in the right direction."

He then handed the princess a slip of paper with the directions to the house were they could meet up and hopefully find what to do next, which the princess carefully packed away in her rucksack.

He then said, "I wish you all the best of luck, and a safe and speedy journey." He handed the princess a package, and took his leave. The princess opened it to reveal some cloaks for them in the style of the ice realm. They took off the ones they were wearing, and put on the ones that would disguise them in the ice realm. They would need both luck and stealth on their side, it seemed, for their next trial.

After the chancellor had left, they were soon notified that the horses were ready. Gathering their rucksacks and following the groom to the courtyard, they saw their horses ready for them.

They were magnificent animals, groomed and tacked in a most elegant manner, although they were war horses, built to carry dragons in armor easily. From their build, one could tell these were draft horses for certain. There were two horses that were of a grayish color, two brown, and one completely white.

After the males of the group had first assisted the female dragons to mount, they then did so, and the princess started off her horse, the white one, at the head of the group.

They rode their horses out of the city, and around the trail that led them along the edge of the great lake, and out of the mouth of the cave that sheltered both it and the city. The horses, being used to more weight than young adult dragons with little to no armor, made rapid strides, and so helped the group to travel to their next stop quickly, far better than the ship.

They continued to make good time, and passed many towns and villages, stopping to eat and rest as they needed. They soon began to notice that the trees of the kind they were used to in the fire realm were becoming fewer here, and in their place, there started to be more evergreen trees. They all wrapped their cloaks the more tightly around them the further they went. The princess wondered how the ice dragons could stand this, being reptiles like they were. Then she thought that, while that was true, it was also true that every type of dragon had the ability to control, and thus protect themselves from, their type's own element.

They realized they must be approaching the border; the temperatures were certainly dropping and not far ahead, snow was falling, as it almost always did in the ice realm, due to the ice dragons' abilities.

They soon came to a sign that did indeed confirm that it marked the border of the fire realm with the ice realm. The dragons took one more look back at the fire realm, and then turned and rode off across the border, not knowing what might await them in the next trial.

CHAPTER EIGHT

The small group, now proceeding on their journey via the large horses that had been lent to them by the chancellor of the fire realm with the fire king's permission, had almost reached their next destination, the capital city of the ice realm. They had been warned of possible encounters there with the agents of the dark dragon, were on alert for anything suspicious, and were once again traveling incognito and in disguise.

They had already changed garments before they entered the new realm; if there was a higher possibility of ambush here, the more the need for caution.

They spied their goal, the sprawling ice palace, with its beautiful and sparkling turrets, carved completely out of gigantic blocks of ice. The ice kingdom's flag, with colors of blue and white, were tossed about in the high winds that so often churned up blizzards here.

A recent snow had fallen, and so their horses had some difficulty making their way through the streets towards the palace. Although it was day, there were few out and about in the streets, but that was not uncommon for the ice realm. That didn't mean it was small. In fact, it was one of the most populous realms, but one would never be able to tell that simply by comparing the activity in the streets of the various realms.

They knew, however, that it would not be easy to

enter the ice palace now. The ice kingdom had already nearly fallen to Laubadar's forces, and in any event he still occupied the realm. They had been directed to a small house where there was a secret room underground where the remnants of the rebellion were now housed. It was to their leader that they were to speak to get intelligence, at least as up to date as could be for the moment, and also advice on how to get past the guards of the palace, which consisted of dragon-lichs and shadow-lichs alike.

The five dragons approached the door, knocked, and gave the password, which the chancellor of the fire kingdom had also given them. They had already stabled their horses a few houses up, and had taken the route around the outskirts of the city to hopefully avoid detection. Upon the last of the group entering, they were led down into the secret chamber.

When he saw them, the leader of the rebellion approached.

"Well, I must say that I am glad you all have made it here safely, but I only wish that it were in better circumstances for our realm and the others."

"Indeed. We were told you might have news, and advice, for us."

"Well, I have some good news and some bad news."

"What's the bad news?" the princess said, the feeling in her stomach saying she wanted to get that over with as quickly as possible.

"Well, I'm afraid that there might be no way to complete your mission here in the ice realm with Laubadar occupying it, at least not now."

"What do you mean?"

"Well, we don't have underground passages, like they do in the fire kingdom, so there's no way for you to get around undetected here."

When the princess gave him a look, as if to ask how he knew about that, he replied "I used to be a member of the court here in the ice realms. While the common citizens of the realms don't know about things such as that, diplomats that go between kingdoms usually do, and I was a high ranking diplomat to the fire realms."

"Anyway," he continued, "there's one other issue besides that. Laubadar, although he hasn't turned his eye back on the ice realm fully, due to the issues he's encountering with his invasion of the fire realm, he sent his second-in-command, a dragon named Arkdhar, to hold the palace and hunt down the rest of the resistance here. As long as he occupies the palace, you could all be in danger as long as you're here. That's not even mentioning how you'd get past the shadow-lichs to get inside."

"There is still some good news, though." He went on. "It appears that Laubadar is yet unaware of your exact mission, in other words that you are really after the maps instead of the weapons right now. If you could find a way to get in and find what you need without being detected, it would be to your advantage to keep it that way. Oh, and there's one other thing. Before he was captured, the king of the ice realm gave this to me, and asked me to make sure it got to you."

He brought out a letter and handed it to the princess. She quickly opened it and began to read.

"To the group from Rhodran"

CHRONICLES OF RHODRAN

"I must put this down and entrust it to one of my court to get to you in case I am captured. If I cannot be there to tell you myself, I have to tell you this somehow.

I am aware that, if I should be captured, it will likely not be easy to gain access to the palace, however, if you do find a way to gain entry, here is what you need to know:

The test of the ice realm is hidden in a secret chamber beneath the ice palace. One must enter it through the throne room. There is a trapdoor in the floor through which you must enter the chamber.

If you pass the test, the way to get the map will reveal itself to you. Good luck on the trial, and good luck on the mission, for the sake of all the realms.

One last thing that might be helpful to you: if you should have been discovered or otherwise run into *trouble and need some assistance in getting to the next realm after passing the test and getting the map piece, I have an old friend who lives near the border that touches the earth realm. He lives in a cave near the border, but you can see it from the road. I recommend you go see him if you need some help, and he'll help you as best as he can, if I'm not able to.*

Karvarthuk, King of the Ice Dragons"

"How are we supposed to get past the shadow-lichs and Laubadar's second-in-command to get to the throne room?" the princess mused.

Before anyone could answer, however, they all heard noises coming from the house above. The guard who stood at the top of the stairs beside the secret entrance in the house above signaled down that it was shadow-lichs and the second-in-command.

The leader quickly ran over to a wall, pressed a panel, and it opened up to reveal a shaft with a ladder. He said, "This is our emergency exit. Hurry! Get out through here! It leads to the house next door to the one you entered. Go out the back door there, and get to the palace. We'll hold them off here as long as we can. You should have enough time to get to the throne room and find the chamber."

As the last of the group entered the shaft, and the leader of the rebellion closed the panel after them, they heard a crash. The shadow-lichs had seemingly found the secret door into the hideout.

The small band of five quickly pushed open a trap door in the house next to the one they had been in. The princess stopped, and turned back as they were turning to leave for the back door.

"What's wrong, Your Highness?" asked the mage.

"It's just...I hate to just leave them there. Isn't there anything we can do? There must be something we could do."

"Unfortunately," said the knight, "I don't think there is. The leader told us to run. I think it'd be even worse for them if we were there with them, and we would just end up getting captured, too. That would be the end of it if we were taken trying to help them; they would have no hope. There would be no one left to do what we're doing, to complete our mission."

The princess sighed, and looked one more time towards the trap door. Then, the group ran towards the back door of the house, slipping out as silently as they could.

They climbed up onto the roofs of the next row of

houses over, and glided low to the palace to avoid being spotted. They landed in front of the gates, and entered. In the first foyer, they found a few shadow-lichs that had apparently been left behind to guard the palace.

This was their first real look at the lichs that Laubadar could create. Some of them were dragon-lichs and some of them were shadow-lichs.

The dragon-lichs, which they knew had been transformed from dragons, simply seemed to be rotting combinations of flesh and bone. They retained their agility and intelligence, however, and yet it seemed that they also were more bestial, as they walked on all fours again, as the dragon ancestors had.

The shadow-lichs, as well, seemed bestial, as they too moved on all fours, but were almost insubstantial and hard to hit. To look at them, they seemed to be nothing more than writhing shadows, but they were perfectly capable of wrapping shadowy appendages around you, pulling you down or holding onto you. They also had the ability, unlike the dragon-lichs, of disappearing and reappearing anywhere else they wished, in a wisp of smoke and shadow.

The mage muttered an incantation that she had never tried before, and a bright light glowed at the tip of her staff. She let it charge, then it expanded to blast and stun the lichs.

"There, that should take care of them, temporarily, at least. Let's hurry, before the others and the second-in-command come back." the mage encouraged them onward.

They ran down the main corridor, and soon came to the throne room. They spotted the throne and raced towards it. Behind it, they did indeed find the trapdoor, all of the group got through it, and the last shut the trapdoor behind them again.

Down this shaft, at the bottom of the ladder, they found themselves in an ice chamber, covered seemingly from ceiling to floor in inscriptions of various types.

"Now, this is my kind of test. Let me get to work seeing what these say." the scholar said, and they swore they could almost see a smile on his face.

Soon he had deciphered the chamber.

"Alright, here's what it said, as far as I can tell. It gives the rules and explains the contest. You see those three paths over there? If you couldn't decipher the language, you wouldn't know which one to use. It says that you must use your knowledge to find the correct path, and there are three chambers, not counting this one. In each chamber, there will also be a keyword that is in the writings, and in the final chamber, you have to give all three to pass the test."

They had soon continued through all the chambers, their lantern's light gleaming off of the icy walls of the chambers and passages. The scholar dragon had read carefully through all the inscriptions in various languages in each chamber to ensure that he got both the correct route to the next chamber and the correct keywords to pass the trial.

In the last chamber, they saw a door instead of a passageway, directly across from them on the opposite wall.

The scholar walked up to it and studied it. He saw what to do and tapped the carvings that matched the three keywords in the other chambers.

The door opened to let them pass. They entered and found another chamber, this one containing the second map piece.

"Well," remarked the scholar. "He did say that once you pass, the way to the map would be revealed."

They tucked the second map piece into the journal in the scholar's rucksack and, since there was no other way to go but back, they headed back down the same corridors to the chamber that had the shaft with the ladder that led back up to the throne room.

They agreed to proceed carefully. The group had no idea how much time the rebels had been able to buy them, keeping the forces of Laubadar busy so they could pass the test and find the piece of the map. The scholar agreed to go up the ladder first, and the others follow. He stopped at the top of the ladder, with the others below, and carefully lifted the lid a bit.

The scholar carefully poked his head out from under the trap door. He was looking and listening intently for any indications of anyone nearby. He could hear nothing, so he gently put the lid all the way down and climbed out. He pressed himself up behind the back of the ice realm's throne, and listened again. He peeped around the throne to see.

There was no one in the throne room, at least for the moment. They were either still at the house fighting the rebels, or else had captured them and were securing them down in the dungeons. He leaned over the trapdoor and motioned the others to come up. When they all had, they closed it again.

They made their way across the throne room and to the door. Once there, they carefully checked to see if anyone was outside. The mage cast some spells for concealment and cloaking, but while they would be all but invisible, they could still be sensed by other means, and if they were, the spell would be rendered useless.

They saw no one coming, so they started down the hall, passing the corridors that led off to the left and the right.

Soon, though, they heard some voices coming down a side corridor, and so bolted to another one, the next one down the hall, and hid there in the shadows. They could hear the two servants talking as they passed.

"Yeah, those new prisoners they're securing in the dungeons ought to be glad that Laubadar's not here, since he's busy taking care of the fire realm personally."

"They won't be so lucky for long. Laubadar says he doesn't expect the fire realm to hold out much longer, and when it's finally under his control, they'll be next in line for joining his army of dragon-lichs."

The two walked off, still talking. The group headed towards the door, hoping that with everyone busy in the dungeons, they might be able to get out unnoticed.

They had almost reached the door, and were entering the foyer where the front doors were, when their luck just didn't hold out.

One of the shadow lichs that had been looking in another direction as they passed turned quickly and alerted the others. It apparently had better senses than the others, and detected and backed them up against a wall. As soon as it had called the others, they appeared in smoke around it. The spell had dissipated by that time, revealing them.

A few moments later, the second-in-command of

Laubadar came in as well, apparently one of the last ones back from the raid.

"Well, my pets," he chuckled, "what have you found now? More of the rebels? They can easily join the others in the dungeons."

As he was walking towards them, the knight and the mage nodded to each other under their hoods, and in a flash of light, the knight was gone.

But not for long. He reappeared, and almost too quick for the eye to see, had drawn his sword. Arkdhar, however, was also very quick and the two swords rang as they clashed against each other.

The knight looked back at them for a split second, and saw the scholar was lashing out at the lichs that had started attacking, and managed to defeat a few, who simply disappeared into smoke. The mage was keeping a light at the tip of her staff, as well as sending out a few blasts of magic here and there. The princess and Eordwar were getting in a few good strikes with their daggers.

The clashing of swords continued amidst the sounds of growling from the lichs, and the thumps and blasts of magic from the group that were fighting them.

The shadow-lich who had found them, who seemed to be the leader of the pack that now overran the former palace of the ice realms, reared up and charged at the princess. All he got for his efforts was a bash across the head with the scholar's staff and a blast of light from the staff of the mage.

Both types of lichs seemed to be far more vulnerable to the light than the weapons, although they were somewhat effective, the mage and the scholar seemed to be having more luck because their weapons were not close-range.

The dragon knight unleashed his fire breath to encircle them to draw his opponent in close range. The fight between them ended soon after when the knight managed to grip his sword tightly and bash the pommel right into the jaw of the other dragon. Arkdhar fell to the floor, unconscious.

As if this was the cue, the mage let out a giant blast from her staff once more, and that seemed to knock out the remainder of the dragon-lichs and dissipate the shadow-lichs.

However, such commotion did not go unnoticed, and they could hear the sounds of many of the other sentinels in the palace coming their way.

The mage took a deep breath, and muttered an

enhancing incantation, and then started the spell to teleport them away. They disappeared from the palace and reappeared in the stable where their horses were.

The group quickly untied them and rode off. They had fortunately not undone any of their tack before, just tied the horse's reins and fed them. They made a hasty retreat, now that the snow had packed down from the cold temperatures of the day. The town had no walls, at least to the front, the mountain that had originally housed the ice dragon tribe looming over and surrounding part of the city at its base; the mountain's caves that had originally housed the ice dragons having long ago been abandoned to build a new, more spacious capital.

As soon as they were out of the city, they took to the forest trails, which would help to hide them somewhat, as the lichs often chose to cover more ground by flying and searching for their targets from the air, rather than on foot, and the tree cover would help to hide the trail. However, they would probably not be chasing them for a while yet; they had beaten back and defeated a lot of the lichs, which would probably take some time to recover, regroup, and begin the chase.

They rode in silence, but the scholar was the first to break it with a question.

"Why didn't you tell us you could do that?" he asked, turning to the mage. "I mean the teleporting thing. We might have been able to just..."

"Teleporting is not that easy, especially with larger groups," the mage explained, still winded from the effort, "it not only takes an enhancing spell, but the teleport spell itself is complicated and takes a lot of energy. I probably won't be able to do that again for a while, but it was necessary for that moment. Desperate times and all that."

The little band rode in silence most of the rest of the way, each of them thinking in their own way about what had happened, and what they had lost.

The princess, for her part, still regretted that they had been unable to assist the rebels; perhaps if they had, those citizens of the ice realm might still be free, instead of locked up in the palace, awaiting their fate at Laubadar's claws.

The knight, meanwhile, was thinking about the opponent he had just faced. He had won, and held him off, but it had been close. The fight had been much tougher than anticipated. It was fortunate that he had gotten the element of surprise by using his fire powers.

The mage was thinking about whether or not she'd

made the right decision, weakening herself for a fair amount of time by using up so much energy like that in the escape attempt.

She felt she would be lucky to have recovered enough by the time that it was time for her trial, but she had no other choice. Not doing everything she could to help them escape was not an option. She would just have to rest as much as possible before the trial where she would have to test her magic skills in the water dragon's realm.

The other two males, while they had been able to help, mused about their abilities as compared with the others, and wondered how to be the most effective they could in battles.

All five of the dragons took some heart, however, in the fact that they had made good their escape, and that they had completed the trial and retrieved the map before they did so. It had taken a lot of effort, but they had been up to the challenge, and if the time came, they would do whatever was necessary to make sure they were up to the next.

The five dragons spotted the cave that the friend of the ice dragon king was supposed to live in, and turned off the road to ride up to it. The snow was hard packed, as it was everywhere that there wasn't a fresh snowfall, and so they tied their horses to trees at the tree-line of the forest, and walked up the hill to the cave.

Inside the cave as they entered sat an elderly, blue dragon who came and greeted them.

"I can't say I get many visitors out here, being so far away from the capital. I also know that there are few in this kingdom who have yet escaped capture. What is it that you travelers need my help with?"

"It was suggested by the ice realm's king to come here for your advice, and we could also use a place to shelter for the night." the princess requested.

"And you'll have both, as much as I am able to give them. Come inside, and make yourselves at home."

The five of them all sat down by the fire he had going, glad for the warmth after hours of riding in the cold wind.

"Well, I'm afraid that I won't be much help in terms of any news, I don't usually get that all the way out here, but I'll help in any way I can."

"There is one major thing," the dragon knight spoke up. "Do you know any ways to keep the lichs from finding you? We still have to cross the border, and until then, we need to keep them off our trail."

"Are you kidding?" the old dragon chuckled, "How do you think I get by way out here? Of course I know ways to avoid them. Well, the first thing is, they tend to go by smell, so if you can mask your scent, you can mask your trail, at least from them, but they tend to send a sentry with them, to take charge of any prisoners they might find."

After thanking the old dragon for his help, they laid down and rested until a short time before daybreak. Having decided that they needed to move on quickly as possible to the earth realm, they took their leave and took advantage of the low light before dawn to cover their departure.

Soon they could tell that the ground was becoming less snowy, and some vegetation was showing, just as it had in the fire realm. The trees, grasses, and shrubs were showing up again, and were now thicker. The border with the earth realm was just ahead. Without looking back, they rode across to the next challenge, knowing that once they completed their mission, the rebels that had supported them would once again be free, as would all the realms.

CHAPTER NINE

As the determined dragons rode onward towards the capital of the earth realm, they noticed how it seemed different from any of the other realms they had been in. The horses had an easier time covering ground here, even more so than in the fire realm. Whereas there the ground was not level, it was rocky and uneven in places, here in the earth realm, it had a lot of level fields full of the produce of the earth, both cultivated by the citizens and not.

The group relaxed a little, knowing that they

shouldn't have to worry as much about a large group of sentries and lichs pursuing them now, but that didn't discount that there could very well be smaller groups or single agents sent after them to track them and disrupt their activities.

Fortunately, they hadn't left the old dragon's lair empty-handed. He had given them some earth realm garb to wear that had been entrusted to him by the king of the ice realm. He had also given them a special potion that, when rubbed on, would dull or eliminate the scent trail they left behind, to make it harder to follow them, at least for the lichs.

The many flower and produce shops in the towns along the way were a testament to how fertile the fields in this particular realm were. That was of course, helped along by the earth dragons' natural abilities, and they did much trade, especially in food items, with the other realms.

Weary with travel, the group finally approached the city gates. They were admitted, and proceeded to the palace. The palace guards saw them approach, and took their horses for them when they dismounted, and announced them to the steward.

"Hello, the king has been expecting you, I'll take you to him right away," the steward informed them when he came out a few minutes later.

He led the five dragons through the halls of the palace, and to a sumptuous throne room. They saw the king on his throne talking to an adviser. He turned to see them, and after sending the adviser to take care of some business, he turned again to see them bowing to him.

"Oh, there's no need to bow," the king remarked,

"especially as one of you is the daughter of the high king. I am glad to welcome you all to my realm. I suspect you can see that, so far at least, we here in the earth realm have been fortunate not to be greatly troubled by Laubadar's forces. I hope that through your mission, and with this trial you have come to complete, that may remain so."

"I know," he continued, "that you are anxious to proceed to your trial, so I will give you the information. It will proceed tomorrow at our realm's stadium, and will be a test of agility and cunning, through the use of an obstacle course. Your champion will need to be quick, agile and cunning to pass this test, and then I will reveal to you the location of the map piece so you may proceed to collect it. Who will be your champion for this trial?"

"That would be me." Eordwar stepped forward.

"I'm the fastest and most cunning, so I'll take on this challenge."

"So be it, then. Part of the test is target practice, so do you wish to use arrows or throw a bladed weapon?"

"I'll use daggers. I'm more used to them than a bow and arrow."

"Very well. We will have the course ready for you first thing tomorrow. Your friends may come and watch, but the champion must complete the trial on his own. No other spectators will be permitted. The course will be timed, but the target practice is scored. The closer you get to each of the five target's center, the higher your score. That, when combined with how many obstacles you successfully overcome, will determine whether you pass. Good luck to you in the trial."

After dining regally that night, the four others,

besides the champion retired to their chambers that they had been assigned, to rest and get ready for the next day. They needed to be there to cheer their champion on.

Eordwar, meanwhile, had asked to be allowed some sort of place to practice for the trial. He was taken to a nearby target range set up just outside the city, and given lots of daggers to use. He might be used to using the dagger in his hand as a weapon, but that didn't mean he was used to throwing it at a target. He didn't seem to hit the target very well at first, but he eventually was able to step back further than required, and be able to hit at least close to the bulls-eye.

After practicing enough that he was satisfied that he could consistently come at least close to the center when he threw the dagger, he started back towards the castle. It was now getting dark, and he needed to rest to be in top condition for the course tomorrow.

True to his word, the king sent his servants to awaken the five dragons nearly at the crack of dawn. They all prepared themselves, and as soon as they were ready, they were lead in procession, with the king at the head as the host of the trial.

He led them through the streets to a large stadium, nearly as large as the one in the fire realm, and through the doors toward the arena area, where the course was set up and the trial would take place.

The king introduced them to a large green dragon, who had bowed to the group as they approached.

"This is my closest adviser, and he will be the referee for this trial. He will observe the champion on the obstacle course, and score the target practice. Only he and the champion are allowed on the field, so I will lead the rest of you up to the seats so we can watch from there."

The others followed the king up some stairs and into the stadium seats. The princess was nervous as she looked to see what kind of obstacle course it was. It looked pretty difficult, but she thought if any of their group could do it, it would be Eordwar for sure.

That very dragon was following the referee onto the arena floor. He got his first look at the obstacle course. It was a long one, with all sorts of obstacles: bars to walk across, things to climb and jump over, and of course, the targets.

"Okay," began the referee dragon, "you'll have a maximum of one hour to complete everything on this arena. When you finish one obstacle, follow the markings on the floor to the next. The course must be completed in order. Points are deducted for each obstacle that is failed or not completed. Step to the starting mark. Use of wings and or flying are not permitted. When you're ready, time will begin. Good luck."

Eordwar stepped forward, folding his wings tightly to his sides. He took a deep breath, and then started off at a run. He could hear the whistle of the referee blow to mark the time.

The first obstacle was a long wooden balance beam that he had to cross without losing balance and falling into the mud beneath. That seemed easy enough, but there were sandbags swinging that he also had to avoid. He slowed down as he approached and carefully started across the bar. He managed, just barely, to get across without falling; though a couple of times he only avoided a sandbag by a hair.

The next obstacle was to climb up a length of rope, which was attached to a wooden wall at the top, and then back down the rope on the other side. This was followed by using a rope to swing across a pit without falling in.

In the next obstacle, Eordwar had to run a zig-zag pattern around some poles without touching them, and then climb up a rock wall and back down. When he had completed that, he could see the next one: cross a log without falling in a pool of water. For this one, the log would move and twist under the challenger's feet, so one had to be very quick and agile to avoid falling in. He succeeded in this as well, and saw the last obstacle: the target range.

There were five targets there, lined up, and the throwing line was marked. He took the five daggers that were laying there for him, and slipped them all in his belt. He walked to the line for the first target, drew a dagger, and threw. It missed the center, but came close. The second hit the bulls-eye, the third didn't, but again came close. The fourth hit the center, too. Eordwar took a deep breath now. This was the last one. He drew the last dagger out, and walked to the line. He focused all his attention on the center bulls-eye, drew back his arm and threw. It hit dead center!

"Well, since you hit three out of five here, let me score these, and I'll be with you shortly to give the results."

Eordwar went up into the stands to sit with his friends while they awaited the results.

"My boy, I must say that was astounding. You must be skilled with daggers indeed to hit three out of five dead center." the king complemented him.

"It's like I said, I'm just used to them."

"Alright," said the referee as he approached, "I have the results now. With the obstacles cleared, and the scores from the three targets that you hit dead center, and the points from the other two, you have officially passed the obstacle course trial."

"Congratulations, my boy," said the king, slapping him on the back, "Let's all go back to my palace to celebrate, and then I'll tell you all about where you need to go next."

When the group had all eaten their fill, the king began to explain.

"If you ride out of the city, a little further on there's a forest. In the middle of that forest, there is a large tree. If you have a mage, then they can find the spell that will cause the tree to reveal carvings. You have to read and follow the directions on those carvings to locate the map piece."

The five dragons called for their horses to be saddled and made ready, and soon they were once again on the move, this time to the forest.

It was a peaceful place, shady, but not as thickly canopied as the one they had seen on the seer's island. The kind of place that was good for a long, leisurely ride through the cool of the shade.

They had soon come upon the tree in the middle of the forest. The mage began the incantations, and sure enough, the tree slowly began to show its carvings. When they had appeared, the scholar dismounted and began to decipher their meaning. He scribbled down some notes on a piece of parchment, and as soon as he had the entire message fully understood, he told the mage she could release the spell.

She did so, and at that the carvings disappeared, seemingly melting back into the trunk of the tree.

"So, here's what we need to do," the scholar began, "the instructions say that there is a series of trees, like this one, that will lead you to a cave where the map piece is. You have to do, whatever magic it is she did, and the trees will show an arrow. Follow all the arrows, and you'll find the cave."

The group dutifully followed the mage, as she used her senses to detect where the trees were, and to reveal the arrows. Very soon they came upon what must be the cave they sought. The mage released the protective spells, and they all entered.

The cave was much like the other two, and while the scholar read the carvings yet again, it simply didn't present any new information.

The scholar then took up the map piece, another piece of parchment, this one seeming to be the bottom left of a map, the other two they had collected being the top left and top right, and stored it away in the great royal mage's journal with the other two.

He put the journal back into his pack, and they were just about ready to leave. They were interrupted, however, by hearing the neighs of their horses, that seemed to be startled.

None of them liked the feel of this situation, so they made their way to the mouth of the cave carefully to get a look at what was causing the disturbance.

There they saw why their horses had been so spooked. Surrounding them, but not doing anything other than frightening them, they saw the shadow-lichs waiting for them.

"Why do you think they're just standing there?" the princess asked.

The scholar replied, "More than likely because they think they have us checked. They're waiting for us to come out and want to prevent us from reaching the horses to escape."

"Do you think these are the same ones we encountered before?" the princess inquired.

"Probably not, as it seems Laubadar has small bands of them in every realm, even the ones he hasn't gotten control of yet. These are likely one of those small scouting bands, left here to deal with threats like us."

"Well," the mage chimed in, "they're not as in control as they think. I may not be fully recovered yet, and I did use some energy on those spells earlier, but I can still get in a few good blasts. Just don't count on me to teleport again yet."

"Hold on, that might not be necessary," said the dragon knight, looking around. He spied a medium sized rock and picked it up.

"What are you doing?" asked the rogue.

"You'll see." The dragon knight crept to the door and looked out. Good. They were still not really paying attention to the mouth of the cave.

The knight hurled the rock at the closest shadow lich, and dodged back behind the side of the mouth of the cave.

The beast gave a grunt and a growl, which let the knight know he had hit his mark.

It quickly turned to glare at the cave mouth, but could see nothing there. It then turned to glare at the nearest of its fellows, but did nothing.

The knight looked to see what had happened, and then threw another rock. This time, the beast had had enough. It immediately turned on the nearest one, letting out a chilling shriek, and soon every shadow-lich in the group was in a growling, kicking, biting cloud of dust, and moving away from the group of horses.

The knight signaled to the others to make a break for the horses, and they did so.

The five of them had just reached the horses, mounted, and started off, when unfortunately, one of the shadow-lichs turned and saw them. Although it took the beast a moment to get the others to pay attention to it and stop fighting, and by that time the group was some ways away, the shadow-lichs still had the advantage of being faster. They indeed caught up soon, and were not far behind, due to their ability to move swiftly by turning into smoke and shadow.

"I think you just ended up making them mad. Any more bright ideas?" the rogue called out to the dragon knight.

The knight didn't respond; he was too busy trying to stop one of the lichs that had jumped up into the trees, and was clawing, jumping and leaping his way from tree to tree to follow them. The beast jumped, and was about to land on the knight and his horse, when the knight swung his mace, and the lich dissolved in a shower of smoke from the blow.

"I don't know if he has any, but I sure do." the mage replied. "We'll do what I said at first. We need to stand and fight."

The remainder of the pack, despite several hard kicks from the horse's hooves, was still doggedly pursuing them, snapping at the heels of the horses.

"I think the mage is right." the princess gave the order. "We can't very effectively use our weapons in this forest, but I see the edge of the forest, and then the clearing. Once we get there, we'll turn our horses to stand and fight."

The group quickly reached the edge of the forest, and entered the clearing, quickly wheeling their horses around to face their pursuers.

The shadow-lichs didn't seem to know what to make of this, and slowed to a halt. In response, the five dragons halted their horses.

The beast who seemed to be the leader of the lichs made a decision to make the first move.

It lunged forward, and the other remaining lichs followed. The dragons drew their weapons and braced themselves.

When the two groups met and clashed, the knight was seen furiously swinging his mace, hitting their weak spot, the head. The princess, scholar, and rogue were all using their weapons to slash and give blows to any lich that got close enough.

The mage was once again relying on the weakness to light that these creatures always showed. The tip of her wand was lit brightly, and the spells she used once again sent out blasts of magic that seemed to weaken the lichs enough for the others' weapons to finish them off.

The dragon knight finished off the last one, and it dissolved like all the others. The group rested, panting, for a few minutes to regain their energy and then moved on.

At the gates of the city, the weary travelers saw a throng of citizens waiting for them, cheering. Apparently they had their skirmish close enough to the city that it had drawn spectators.

"That was amazing! How did you do that?" one of them called.

"Well," the knight called back, "we've had a few other encounters with those beasts, so I guess we've just gotten used to it."

The going was slow back to the palace, as the crowds insisted on accompanying them back to the king. They were only left in peace when they reached the palace and the gates were shut behind them.

The grooms once again took their horses, and led them away to the stables. The exhausted dragons made their way to report to the king and then arrange for their departure to the next realm.

The king, however, insisted that they were in no shape to go anywhere until tomorrow, at least, and that they should at least get food and rest before then. There would be plenty of time to discuss those arrangements later. The five agreed, and although they could barely keep themselves awake, made a pretty short work of the meal set before them, and then went to their assigned rooms.

After having rested for the night, the earth realm's king once again met with them to discuss their arrangements for travel.

"Firstly," he began, "there's the matter of your horses. They can't go with you to the water realm, they wouldn't be much use to you on an island, anyway. However, I think I might have a solution to this dilemma. I was pondering this last night, and I can offer to have them transported to wherever you need to go after you complete the last trial. Look, you're going to the water realm next, right? As soon as you find out where the weapon's location is, let me know."

"I know," the king continued, "that you have promised to give these horses back to the fire realm's king, and that's where you'll be going to face Laubadar, most likely. So, I'll send them to the realm where the objects are located, and you can just ride them from there. I'll send them with my own merchants, they go to the other realms all the time, and I promise they'll treat them as if they were their own, and get them there safe and sound."

"I have to say, it does seem like your idea is the best," the princess replied. "Okay, so we'll have you send our horses on for us. We still need to arrange a ship to the water realm."

"Oh, that's no problem at all, Your Highness," the great dragon chuckled. "I'll have my men ready one of my own vessels; it'll be the quickest and easiest way there. It should be ready by this evening. In the meantime, take advantage of what the palace and the capital city have to offer."

"Thank you, Your Majesty, for your kind offer. I believe we'll take you up on that."

After taking their leaves of the king, they decided what they would do for the rest of the day. While the princess, the knight, and the rogue decided to head out and view the sights in the city, the scholar and the mage decided to study in the library some more. It was just too tempting an opportunity to pass up, they said.

So, leaving their companions in the palace to read, the three dragons left and first headed, at the knight's suggestion, to the public square. He reasoned that if there were any news, that would be the place to find out.

The dragons had donned their cloaks again, so this time they weren't mobbed as they had been before. They spent some time in the square, but no new information seemed to be available.

Upon leaving, the decision was made to go to the market here, and see if anything caught their eye. They wandered for quite a while, and just as the princess was beginning to think that there would be nothing there either, a small stall with pets for sale caught her attention.

She found an animal she liked, a small ferret, and the shop owner took it out of its cage for her to see. She bargained with him, and finally bought the animal, cage and all. She then decided she'd arrange for it to be sent to her mother, and she liked the thought that she'd have something to come home to when this journey was over.

The knight, too, had seen an animal he was interested in. He asked the shopkeeper about a hawk, thinking that perhaps this would also provide them an expedient way of sending messages.

"Oh, yes," said the shopkeeper, "this fellow is trained to take messages. I've traveled all over the realms, so I dare say he could go just about anywhere for you."

His decision made, the dragon knight bargained as well, and soon had the hawk and the cage in his possession.

They returned to the castle for the night. The next day the princess arranged for her pet, and the cage of the knight's hawk, to be sent ahead of them back to Rhodran. To test the animal, the knight had sent a message to the water king to let him know they would be coming soon.

The earth realm's king had wisely arranged for his ship to leave that night. The five dragons slipped onboard the craft, and settled in just as the ship was pulling out of port. Since it was one of the king's private vessels, there was no worry about anyone else coming aboard, and the added bonus of leaving at night would help to avert any prying eyes as well.

The tiny band was more than ready to see the last trial done, and grew more and more excited. They were on their way back to the water realm, and soon enough, the last trial would determine the rest of their journey, and their destinies as well.

CHAPTER TEN

Having passed the third test, and secured a ship back to the water realm, the small group of warriors had finally arrived at their destination. They didn't spend any time looking at the sights, as they had the last time they had been here. This would be the final test, and they were all anxious to have it completed and over with.

The guard that the princess and the mage had met before was sent to guide them to the palace. The entire group had once again changed into their cloaks that were of the water realm style.

The young dragons could see the water realm's palace towering ahead. In sharp contrast with the other palaces in the other realms, it was constructed entirely out of blocks of coral that had been brought up from underneath the waves. It still had the same lofty spires and turrets as the other palaces, and the locals said that the coral was just as sturdy and hard to break as the stone that made up most of the other palaces, or the deep frozen blocks of ice that made up the ice realm's palace. Some sharp protruding spikes of coral, especially around the tops of the walls where the sentries walked their patrols, seemed to reinforce the idea that it wouldn't be as easy to besiege this palace as it would first appear.

The water dragons had, of course, chosen this material to honor and represent the waters which surrounded their home. It also honored their elemental powers, and the central role of water in their realm.

After having been led up the hill to the palace, the princess and her escort awaited their audience with the water realm's king, and soon found themselves in his presence, with said king having been alerted to their coming by the message of the dragon knight's hawk.

The king of the water realms was a large blue dragon, wearing regal robes. His scales shone turquoise blue, and a diadem was sitting atop his head. He had an air of ancient nobility. The princess remembered that the water realm had only one change of dynasty since its establishment. The other realms, aside from their own, had already been through several successive dynasties.

"Hello, and welcome to the water realm." the king

began. "As the keeper of the fourth trial, I am your host here, and wish you the best of luck in your endeavors."

"Thank you, your majesty." the princess stepped forward to speak for the group. "May we have the rules for this trial?"

"Certainly. This trial is to test the magical skills of those who would seek the great royal mage's magical objects. It was set specifically because having someone with magical abilities for the protection of the group is a must. The trial itself is held in an immense cavern behind a waterfall. The rest of the group may be spectators along with the referee, but may not interfere or enter the field. There will be two major sections of the trial, one will be to test the mage's offensive skills, and the second will be to test the individual's defensive magic. The first part consists of a series of magical duels with some of our realm's best mages. The best two out of three wins. Need I remind you, though, that our realm produces some of the best mages of all the realms? As for the second part, that will consist of standing in the arena while beasts are released into the area, and the champion must use protective and defensive spells to prevent the beasts from harming him or her for a set amount of time, after which the beasts will be recalled, and the test will end."

"Man, and I thought I had it bad when I just got an obstacle course." said Eordwar to the dragon knight, who nodded in response.

The princess glared at both of them to silence them, and turned back to the king.

"We understand, Your Majesty."

"Now that the rules are established, whom do you chose for your champion for this trial?"

"I will be the champion for this trial," stated Targarma, stepping forward.

"Very good. Now, due to the particular nature of this trial, you are allowed to ask for a delay if you so desire. If not, we can proceed to hold the trial tomorrow. Do you, champion, wish to ask for a few days' respite?"

"Yes, Your Majesty, I would like to request a delay in the trial."

"So be it. Four days hence, first thing in the morning, I shall come and lead you to the waterfall cavern where the trial will take place. For now, I will have my servants show you to your rooms."

The remaining days until the trial passed quickly. While the four that were not participants pretty much remained in their rooms and sharpened their own skills, the mage spent the time finishing recuperating and brushing up on spells and magic skills.

When the day of the trial began, Targarma felt that she was as ready as she could be. She felt confident that her magic was honed enough.

The king led them out of the city, and into the forest, and on to a large waterfall. The traveling group, including one of the king's court to be the referee, as well as the three opponents that the mage would face, went single file into the cave behind it.

As soon as the last of them had entered, the mages lit the torches on the walls for light. With the light now flooding the area, they could see it was an arena, a smaller one than the others that they had done trials in, but sufficient for the purpose.

The water dragon king led all who were not

participating to the smaller area of seating. The mage, the referee, and the first opponent took their places on the arena floor.

"All right," the referee began, "I will flip a coin to decide who gets to make the first move. The one who correctly guesses gets to go first."

The coin was flipped, and the opponent guessed tails, while Targarma took heads.

"Heads it is," the referee called, "the champion goes first."

The two mages entered battle stance, and the champion mage started. The spells and flashes of light soon came nearly too close together to distinguish, and it was hard to tell who would win.

"What is the goal of a mage's duel, anyway?" asked

Rhodran's princess.

One of the water realm's mages answered her: "To either knock out the opponent, disarm him, or to exhaust the foe from having to dodge your attacks. There's a bit of strategy to it, and sometimes a mage has to switch in the midst of battle as to which of those he intends to do."

The group's mage, being lighter built, seemed to be doing a good job of dodging the opponent's attacks.

Then Targarma bellowed one last incantation that seemed to levitate the staff from the opponent's claws, and toss it quickly over the lines at the side of the arena.

The referee called the match: "The champion has disarmed the opponent, the first match goes to the champion from Rhodran!"

The second match was also very heated, but ended in a draw. Both of the mages had ended up disarming each other at the same time. Since the match was a draw, they had to move on to the third match to determine the winner.

The third mage from the water realm seemed more determined to overpower Targarma than the other two. He cast spells furiously, which fortunately Targarma was able to dodge, although a couple of them were near misses.

The duel dragged on, at least until the opponent tried to end it with a mighty spell that blasted forth from his staff. The other dragons from Rhodran watched as their mage barely rolled out of the way.

She then seemed to take a breath and summon a powerful spell. When the dust cleared, she had knocked out her opponent, and won the third match. The opponent was coming to, and was led to the sidelines by the referee dragon.

The referee announced that there would be a short break, to prepare the arena for the second phase of the test. The champion mage simply sat down on the sidelines of the arena to take a breather.

Soon, all was ready, and the referee said that everyone should make sure and stay clear while the trial was in progress.

Targarma was instructed to take up her position in the middle of the arena, and they would soon release the first few beasts.

When she saw the first come out, she chanted some protective spells first, to keep her from harm, and then put up a barrier spell to keep the beasts out. Now all she had to do was maintain the barrier. The other spells should protect her, even if the barrier was breached, but all this was easier said than done.

As the minutes counted down, they would occasionally release another beast, but it seemed her barrier would hold. One of the beasts, however, had been continuously attacking it, in spite of the magical shocks it had been receiving all the while. She then cast another spell to reinforce the barrier, and this seemed to slow the beast down, at least. He eventually seemed to give up, and let the others keep trying.

The time was called, and even though it had only been about ten minutes, it seemed far longer to the mage.

Targarma was declared the winner of the trial, and the group filed back to the palace to celebrate.

Afterwards, they were informed by the water realm's king how to access the map piece for which they had come.

"The cave you seek is on a very small island just off the coast, just north of here. I will lend you one of our smaller boats to journey there. It should be ready for you all in the morning."

Princess Asvartha lay awake for a long time that night.

Tomorrow, she thought. *The final piece of the map, and it should be in our hands tomorrow. And not long after that, with any luck, this whole situation will be over, and nothing but memories. I'll free my father, and the ice realm. I know it. We almost have everything we need.*

The servants came early the next morning to rouse

them, and the band was led to the boat they would use to get to the island.

It was a smaller, sail powered boat, capable of beaching on a shore, which is probably why it was chosen. It would be quicker to get in and out with such a ship, rather than a larger one that would require the use of the dinghy to get between ship and shore.

Between the dragon knight and the rogue, the five dragons got the ship out of port, catching the wind and waves, and headed towards the island. They had been given the proper navigational equipment, and the scholar was keeping them on course.

The crew of five soon beached their craft on the shore of the island.

"Alright," said the princess, "the king said that there would be another tree in here, with some more carvings, in the middle of the island near a stream, so let's just cut through to it."

The scholar and the mage followed the princess, while Horzkar and Eordwar stayed with the boat to guard it.

Asvartha cut through some of the undergrowth with her dagger, although the path was not that overgrown so as to be impassible.

The trio soon came upon what they sought. The scholar read the runes, and when the mage used the revealing incantation she had used before in the earth king's realm, this time a passage opened.

The princess looked in, and couldn't tell through the darkness just how deep the shaft down the tree's trunk was.

"What do you think?" she asked the others.

"Well, this time, he must have hidden the map piece in a particularly hard to get to cavern. There isn't even an entrance, probably, other than this shaft." the scholar answered.

He looked into the opening himself, when he was done, he pulled his head back out and gave his findings to the others.

"Yes, there's a thick shaft of wood that's been placed across the thickness of the trunk, just above the entrance, that the rope is tied to. The only way up and down the shaft is to lower oneself down the rope."

"We'll have to go one at a time, I guess. I'll go first."

The mage lit her staff, and tied it to her pack. It

would help light the way down. Following the light, the princess and the scholar grabbed the rope and lowered themselves down, as carefully as they could.

Even with the beacon of the light ahead, or rather below them, it was still dark, and they could tell that the sides of the shaft had not opened out any considerable amount. They had to keep their wings pinned very closely to their sides to make their way down.

Finally, after a seemingly interminable amount of time of getting down the shaft, they heard the mage, just ahead of them, say that she had reached the bottom.

When the others had joined her, she enhanced the spell to increase the light and let them see what was around them.

When their eyes adjusted, they saw a chamber

similar to the ones before, however, when the scholar checked the inscriptions, as he always did, this time he said they gave more information. The map pieces, when put together, gave not only the location of the magical objects they needed, but a password to access the test as well.

The scholar then picked up the last of the four map pieces, and put it in the journal with the others.

"We'll have to study the maps more in depth when we return." he said. "For now, though, let's get out of here."

The three began climbing again, this time being much more difficult than descending, at least until they had reached the ceiling of the chamber again, and the tunnel closed back in on them, so they could prop themselves against the walls of the shaft and use the rope to pull themselves up.

When they reached the entrance in the hollow tree trunk, the mage climbed out first, and held her staff through the entrance to give the others light. When the princess and the scholar had exited, she sealed the entrance again.

They noticed it was almost dark by this time, so they lit their lanterns to help them find their way back.

When the other two dragons saw them coming, Eordwar couldn't help but tease them.

"Finally! We thought you guys had gotten lost, and were wondering if we should come and look for you."

"We got what we came for," the scholar informed them, "it's just that it took us a while longer because it was down a very thin shaft to the chamber."

The three dragons then saw that the other two had lit a fire while they were waiting. "I think we should just stay here for tonight and wait until sunrise to leave." the knight said. "It's harder to navigate at night; sure you have the stars, but there's no moon out tonight."

So they all gathered around the fire, and when they were tired, they all laid down in the boat to rest. They were awakened by the sunrise, and put out the ashes of the fire, preparing to leave. All five of them helped to push the boat back into the water, and when all were back aboard the boat, they unfurled the sails, letting them catch the wind. They steered it back to the south, and around to the port.

After announcing themselves again to the king, and requesting his permission to stay a few days to study the map pieces and what information they might contain, they all retired to their rooms to begin the work of deciphering the map to find the right location.

Up in their rooms, it was not long before they had pieced together the map, the four pieces of parchment fit together again exactly as a larger map, and they could see all the realms.

When they put the map together, the lines began to glow, and there were dots of blue light in each of the realms.

"Wait a minute," said Rordgur, "I recognize these places. These four here, in the fire, ice, earth, and water realms, are where we found the map pieces."

"Then what does this one in Rhodran mean?" the princess asked him.

"I think that must be where the objects themselves are. I don't know if that's where the royal mage hid the test for them, but I'd be willing to wager that's where they are."

"Wait a minute, I think I see...yes, yes, I see some clear signs that there is magical writing." said the mage.

The glow had lasted for a few minutes, but now died down.

"Why do you think it did that?" the scholar asked the mage.

"So that the finders of the map could know where it is, but not anyone else who might be sneaking around after them."

"So what were you saying about the magical writing?" the scholar continued.

"Magical writing is used by mages," Targarma replied, "in the same way that coded writing is used by everyone else. To keep those not in the know from reading something they shouldn't. I would suspect that this is information the royal mage never gave to anyone else. However, like coded writing, it can be hard to crack. There are basic spells, like I was using to make the inscriptions show up, but that will never work with something like this."

"So this is one more hurdle to finding the objects?" the princess asked.

"Yes, Your Highness, but not for long. I'll go down to the library and study the strongest revealing spells they have. I'll have this thing deciphered, one way or another." the green dragon mage assured her.

The scholar was excited at the opportunity as well, and his eyes grew big as he entered.

"I just can't believe they gave us access to the

library here. It's even more extensive than the one in Rhodran. This is a once-in-a-lifetime opportunity for those of us who deal with books and the like. I wonder what I should look at first? Oh, I know, I'll try to see if they have any of the newest maps of the realms. Comparing them to this one might show any changes that might give us a clue as to where the exact location was that it was trying to show us."

They trundled back upstairs with armfuls of books, and all of them began to read, with the scholar and the mage telling them what to look for, but so far, they weren't having much luck.

"Could you make it light up again?" the princess asked the mage.

The mage uttered an incantation, and the lines glowed again. The princess looked at the map where

Rhodran was. The objects were in her homeland. The princess couldn't help but worry that this meant her home would eventually become a target for Laubadar.

Far away, in his great fortress, that very dragon was fending off a long siege from the fire realm's king. He was currently in consultation with his generals. By all appearances, he was also very much not happy.

The dark dragon practically exploded at a suggestion of one of his generals to be patient for the outcome a while longer and continue ahead with their current plans. "What do you mean, 'wait a little longer'? I've been doing nothing but waiting! All we need to do is march out there and end this siege!"

"With all due respect, sir," said his chief general, "the besieged party usually has the upper hand in a long siege, but only if they maintain their advantage and stay inside the walls. We can't fight them in close quarters like that, they're already right up against our walls, and we're just keeping them from attacking or scaling them."

Laubadar growled. "I can just send out some more shadow-lichs to drive them back."

"They seem to have adjusted to that strategy, and are pretty effective at battling the lichs, and besides, those beasts are even less maneuverable than the sentries."

The discussion carried on, while down in the dungeon, the king of Rhodran was considering his options. The siege had never created enough distraction to draw them to send the dungeon guards to the front, so the prisoners had never had a good chance to escape yet. Not to say that they weren't remaining vigilant for the chance if it came, though. They had continued to communicate, and it seemed that no one had yet heard them, or else hadn't caught on to what they were doing.

As a father, though, he could only wish that he had some more news of his daughter and her group. He knew that they were in action by this point, but he had heard no further news of them since then.

Outside the fortress walls, the siege carried on, and the fire king also held council with his generals. They were soon to run out of food, and although they had the home field advantage, the fire realm was not very productive. They had to import a lot of their food, and the shadow-lichs and dragon-lichs that Laubadar sent out were pretty effectively cutting their supply lines.

"How do we handle this?" the fire king asked his general. "We can't demand that the civilians give up their rations of food to the armies, and our rations won't hold much longer."

"If the army's allotted rations begin to fail, we may have to withdraw, and let them come to us in the capital."

"I don't know," the king mused, "that could work, but maybe not. It would take far too long to withdraw, and his forces would likely be out of the fortress gates and on us before we could even get everyone away."

"If we withdraw under the cover of darkness," the general replied, "it might do the trick. They might not be able to follow us, or it could at least hinder their taking notice of our leaving."

"It would have to be a night with no moon, though, and there isn't one of those until after our supplies are projected to run out." the king answered. "It seems as if it's our only choice though. Send a message via the hawk to the chancellor in the capital, and inform him of our decision. Tell him to be ready to let us in quickly, and prepare to defend the city with us when we return."

A few days later, the plan was put into motion, and after sunset they began to break camp to withdraw to the capital. The moon was out, but it was only a sliver, and they hoped they could effect their movement by the morning. It seemed to be going well at first; they had broken camp and even had about three-fourths of the men away, when one of the sentries finally spotted what they were doing. The remaining men had almost all left when the sentries and lichs were finally mustered and came pouring out of the gates. The king, who had refused to leave until the last man did, was taken in the confusion at the rear of the fire realm's army.

Back inside the fortress, as the guards came by, taking the fire king to his cell, Valwardus could only watch in silence. They had broken the siege. He could only hope that, like in the ice realm, the remainder of the fire realm's army and the resistance fighters could keep the dark dragon busy for a little while longer. There was no telling how long they would hold out, though. The king was even more frightened for his daughter now than before. With the fire realm resistance now pretty much the only thing left, Laubadar could turn his attention to the other kingdoms. He didn't know how far along they were in the trials, or if they had retrieved the objects yet. The only thing he knew now was if they didn't hurry, their enemy would only gain strength by the day.

CHAPTER ELEVEN

After a few more days of research in the library of the water realm, the group seemed to be no further along in decoding the magical writing to find out what the royal mage had wanted to tell whomever got the four map pieces.

The mage had tried several spells, but none of them had worked so far. All of them were getting bleary eyed from reading so much.

Targarma reentered the room from one of her

study sessions, and proceeded to carefully turn over the four pieces of the map. She muttered a low, droning incantation, and gently tapped her staff on the four pieces in succession.

This time, something seemed to be happening; the formerly blank reverse sides of the drawn map came alive with all sorts of characters, of an ancient script. It seemed to light up the area around it, along with the faces of the five dragons studying the script now visible before them.

Quickly the scholar began to record and translate the writing. When he was done, the mage tapped the papers once more, and then the script slowly faded away.

"It's just a good thing that I studied up on the older languages. This seems a particularly ancient one." the scholar mused, a few minutes later. He had seemingly been double checking his translations.

"Anyway, this is the best I can tell as to what the writing was saying."

He handed the mage the writing, and she began to read it aloud to the others.

"To whomever may find this map:"

"First of all, congratulations on succeeding in passing the trials necessary to even be holding these pieces in your hands. If you are in need of this, then the realms are likely in grave danger already. If the worst has happened, and Laubadar has already returned, you will need to follow the location on the front of the map, and find the last of the dots marking the locations of the trials I have set. The last trial will be for the gauntlet and spear that will give you the means to defeat the dark

dragon.

The location referenced is my secret lab in the forests of Rhodran. At first, there would appear to be nothing there more than a room. Likely the one who found my journal didn't even suspect that the trial was there. However, if the mage of the group uses the same spell that they used to reveal the writing on this map, a door will reveal itself, and pressing on the middle script with your staff will open it and break the seal.

From that point on, only a prince or princess of the blood of the rulers of Rhodran may enter and proceed, and none other.

This last trial will be like none of the others you have faced before. The champion will have to find their way through traps designed to test their strategy and endurance. The test will be keyed to whatever element the silver dragon is aligned with.

With that out of the way, I wish to share some advice with those who would defeat the great dark dragon, gleaned from my own experiences.

Always remember that Laubadar's powers are dark magic, which only gains power by spreading fear and rifts between dragons, both as individuals, and amongst all the different types of dragons. The dark dragon is very capable of being defeated if you use this to your advantage and turn it against him. In the absence of those two things, his powers weaken.

Also, never take off those protective collars that I created. They have encased within them a special stone which absorbs dark magic, the same from which I used in the gauntlet and spear to produce the same effect. Indeed, jewels can do the same for all dragon abilities.

Best of luck, although I have no doubt that a team capable of passing these trials will have the qualifications necessary to complete the job."

The mage finished reading, and set the paper down. The others seemed to ponder the words of the royal mage for a few moments.

"I never asked, but that reminded me, what is your elemental ability, Your Highness?" the dragon knight asked the princess.

"I'm aligned with fire abilities," replied the silver dragon, "like many of my bloodline."

"But," she continued, "back to the matter at hand. Now that we have the precise location, we should head there post-haste."

The group went to inform the king of the water

realm that they had found the next location and were in need of transport there.

The five of them soon had another ship to take them back to the realm of Rhodran, and were happy to find themselves putting in to port within a short time.

The queen, the princess's mother, had sent some sentries to meet them with their horses, which had been sent ahead by the king of the earth realm, just as he had promised. The princess looked around and was glad that everyone here, at least, seemed to be happy and safe. She was more determined than ever to keep it that way. Her father had been right, though. Her mother was an excellent regent; she had always seemed to know what to do.

The group decided to waste no time in heading to the location of the objects, and after thanking the guards, they mounted and took off, soon leaving the port city behind.

By the next morning, almost midday, they had reached the mage's lab and tied their horses to a nearby tree.

The mage broke the seals as they went, and they were soon standing in the same room the princess's father had been not many months ago. The mage cast the spell to reveal any writings or carvings, and they were not disappointed. There was a space on the back side of the cave that almost immediately lit up with glowing lines and script.

The mage read the script for a moment, and then tapped a group of characters near the center that was apparently the passcode. The door immediately opened, showing another passageway beyond.

"Alright, princess, this is where you head on by yourself. Be alert, you won't know exactly what you might encounter in there."

"Thank you. I promise I'll be careful." The silver dragon responded.

The princess proceeded into the entrance and down the tunnel, carrying one of the lanterns that they had brought to allow her to see even dimly in the darkness surrounding her.

Boy, thought the silver dragon, *this mage sure likes hiding things in dark and narrow tunnels.*

It didn't take long for the princess to come up against her first challenge. There were a bunch of thick, impossible to pass tree roots tangling in each other and blocking the path.

She used her fire breath to burn them away, and passed on through. She had also had to be aware and careful to avoid any dead end passages off of the main one. Just like the other areas they had encountered, this one seemed to be built along the lines of a maze, or at least to disorient anyone trying to find the right path. She came to a small cavern, where she saw a sleeping beast. She thought she could perhaps sneak by without disturbing it. She tried, but the beast was not as asleep as she had first thought.

The beast awakened, stood up, and then roared its frustration at being disturbed. It reared up on its hind legs for a moment, and then charged.

The princess was able to leap out of the way and let the charging beast hit the wall behind her. It recovered, now even more mad, and charged again. The princess kept avoiding the charges, but realized that she needed to go on the offense.

She started blocking off the beast's path by creating spots of fire with her fire breath. Soon there wasn't much room left. She couldn't use her wings in the small space, so she made a leap over one of the fire breaks and landed on the beast's back.

It tried to buck her, but found that doing so was easier said than done. She grabbed its ears like reins and when it took off, frantically trying to find an opening, she drove it into a wall and knocked it out.

The princess wondered how such a creature could be down here, but she remembered that Targarma had once said that a powerful enough mage could be able to create an illusion of a beast with enough substance to seem real, and that they would act the same, as well. Similar, in fact, to the making of the shadow lichs. It was possible that such a spell had been used here.

The spots of fire were dying out now, not being able to really spread in the sandy, rocky soil of the tunnel, and allowed the princess to continue out of the cavern and on her way. She could only wonder what other traps or obstacles might lay ahead of her before she reached her goal.

The route continued on, leading past several more obstacles, such as a boarded off tunnel, which she cleared once again with her fire breath, and a pit trap, that she almost triggered and fell in. Fortunately she was able to grab some thick roots overhead as the top of the trap collapsed beneath her. At least this tunnel was quite a bit larger than the first part of the passage had been.

She swung herself over to the other side of the pit,

and continued on. Not far up the pathway, she saw a light coming through an entrance.

It was a great cavern, and as she looked up, she could see that the roof had partially caved in, and from there the light was streaming in from above. There were torches on the wall, but they were not lit, and likely hadn't been for a long time.

It looked similar to the other places that they had found the royal mage's maps, but bigger. She looked around to see where the object of their quest was.

She found a niche in the far wall, and as she approached it, she saw she was in luck; the objects were still there. As she admired them, she couldn't tell which of them impressed her more.

The gauntlet was large, at least for a female dragon, but made of brass and intricately decorated and adorned with lots of jewels. There were five larger ones, of different colors, that she supposed were for what the royal mage had said; storing and releasing energy from the elements that the dragons had control over. The most interesting thing about it though, in her opinion, was that the jewels that seemed to be storing energy shone, as a normal jewel would, but those that weren't storing energy were dull. Perhaps this was rather the jewels that were storing the dark energy that the gauntlet absorbed?

The spear, on the other hand, wasn't really adorned with embellishments, the only jewel was on the head, where it attached to the shaft. This one, too, seemed dull. The shaft of the spear itself was also unusual. Instead of being made of wood, it seemed to be made of metal, although hollow and light, and with the ability to retract in sections. The head of the spear was brass, just like the gauntlet, and was almost as tall as her when fully extended for use.

As she packed up the two objects and prepared to leave, she noticed some cracks in the wall near the niche. These she examined, and soon found another passageway. She decided to see where it led. It soon seemed to turn back towards the direction from which she came. Perhaps this was a way back to the mage's lab?

Her suspicions were confirmed when she reached the end of the tunnel. It came out, she found, right near the entrance to the lab.

The others were surprised to see her coming from that direction. They asked her how she had come around that way, as they had expected her to return through the secret passage to the trial.

"Well," she explained to them, "I suppose that Urdharmus must have thought that if you have the objects, you shouldn't have to go back through the traps and trials, so he made another secret way out once you got the objects."

"Perhaps another way to misdirect those with bad intentions." the scholar mused.

"Anyway," Asvartha said, "I know you guys have been waiting to see these. Here they are." She pulled the magical gauntlet and spear from her pack and held them out for the others to see.

The other four each took turns examining and admiring the two ancient objects. They returned them to her when they had all taken a turn.

"Oh, I almost forgot," the scholar blurted out, "Your Highness, there's something we found while you were in there, and it seems to relate to the mission."

"Can you show me?"

The scholar brought her over to a book that was laying open on the table nearby, and she began to read it. The pages were old and worn, but the writing was still legible enough, even if a bit faded. It appeared to be some notes from the royal mage.

"*To be able to defeat an enemy, one must first know one's enemy. As the dark dragon prepares to attack the realm of Rhodran, I have been entrusted by my liege, King Varthulus, to find a way to halt his seemingly unstoppable encroachment on the realms. In light of this, and keeping in mind the above, I began to do exhaustive research into Laubadar the dark dragon, why he is so interested in dark magic as opposed to the magic that almost all other mages ascribe to, and his history. I called on the archives to turn over to me for study everything they had in regards to him, and any research notes that he had, if they had access to them.*

It would seem that, at least at first, he had little ambition. I could almost detect no traces of the dragon he was to become when reading through his first notes. However, for quite some time before the accession of Varthulus, he had begun researching some very ancient lore, relating to how it was believed that the original dragons who showed elemental affinities and abilities were thought to have come to possess them.

After this, he came to look into the methods of absorbing and containing these powers from others. He came to this research after finding out that there was potential for one dragon to contain and be able to use all of the elemental abilities within a single individual. There seemed to be indications that if this were actually to be done, that that one dragon would have great power indeed, perhaps even limitless power.

Despite the fact that not even silver dragons have more than one elemental affinity, and despite the fact that the research itself explicitly said that it would be extremely difficult to pull off; despite the fact that if it were even possible, it would be highly dangerous, still Laubadar continued his line of study.

The notes that I read, in the dark dragon's own hand, continued on to say that this ultimate power, if achieved, was likely to be able to pull off the ultimate objective of necromancy: the bringing of the dead back to life. Even the smaller, less powerful spells of necromancy are all Laubadar needs to create his dragon-lichs and shadow-lichs.

This made me wonder, why would he so single-mindedly pursue this perhaps self-destructive method, why seek to absorb all this power from the living to reanimate the dead? I then turned my attention to the records that the archive had of his history.

He seemed to have had a fairly decent childhood, until he was orphaned by the deaths of his parents to illness when he was a young drake. All the reports up until that time showed that he was a well-liked youth, but that changed when he had to be sent to an orphanage. He was apparently not treated well there, and perhaps came to long for what he had lost. I wondered if that could be why he was so desperately trying to find a way to truly bring the dead back to life?

However, I found, in checking his later notes, that although that might have been a reason that he started, it didn't seem to be his current ambition. His plans, which were ruined by the election of the current king, were to become the head of the lands, and thus have an easier path to the unification of the realms under himself. The dark dragon had spent years under the chieftain as a chief adviser waiting for the moment to make good on his goal. He was, of course, bitter about the outcome that put the silver dragon on the throne instead of him. He held his peace at first, and then struck later. His notes at the time show he had started creating his minions, but his aims were to complete his work, to be able to have a true undying army, with him as an immortal king at its head. He had apparently been creating lichs under the nose of the dragon chieftain who had reigned before King Varthulus.

Perhaps this marked the point that his end ambitions had shifted from regaining what he had lost to gaining revenge on those he thought had wronged him, though I can't be sure. Perhaps the influence of the dark magic that he had been dealing with had corrupted what was once an understandable, if misguided, goal into something incomprehensible?

All I knew for sure was that now I had a more thorough understanding of his goals, I could even use some of his research against him. Sure, dark magic could absorb the elemental abilities of dragons, but there were also ways to absorb dark magic from Laubadar.

I hastened to apply myself and discover a way to absorb and contain his dark magic, to protect the realm and to put an end to his threat. I found that it could be effectively contained within certain stones, along a similar concept to Laubadar's early experiments of trying to contain the elemental powers in orbs.

I crafted the gauntlet and spear using stones I had

specially enchanted to absorb, conduct and contain dark magic. I knew without his powers, he would be helpless. If he had carried out his plan to drain the elemental powers from the dragon kings, which I knew he could not until he had the kings captive, it would still be able to absorb and contain that from him, and return it to its rightful owners.

I am probably the only one who has researched this matter so deeply, and Laubadar likely believes that no one knows his true intentions, but with this knowledge and hopefully the element of surprise, I will be able to overpower him."

The princess turned back to the scholar, still pondering over what she had read. She didn't quite know what to make of it, any more than the royal mage had, but it gave her at least some more insight into how everything came to pass.

"And that's not all, either, Your Highness," the scholar said to the silver dragon, as he turned the pages back to a different section of the book. "This appears to record some notes on Laubadar's lair. We had already read all this while we were waiting for you to return, but we thought it would be useful for all of us to know."

The silver princess turned back to the book, and began once again to read the royal mage's notes.

"The treacherous mountain lair that the dark dragon Laubadar calls home is fitting to him in more ways than one. It is constructed out of a mountain made almost entirely out of a very jet black obsidian stone. This is a stone that is well known for having properties that easily dampen all other elemental abilities, while somewhat amplifying dark magic.

This allows him to take the advantage against any

who try to encounter him there, however there are certain ways to counter these effects. The dampening effect on dragon abilities is also not total, so there is still some leeway to use one's natural abilities, even if one must face the dark dragon in his own lair.

One such way is to reduce the use of one's abilities, and rely more on carried weapons. This is part of why I created the trials, so that whomever might need to face him would at least have some practice in proficiency with manual weapons, rather than totally depending upon their elemental powers.

Another way is to use one's powers in combination, to achieve maximum effects. Fire abilities work well with ice, for instance, if water is necessary. That in turn can even the odds.

The power dampening effect also does not affect

any inanimate objects. The gauntlet and spear will still function at full power, and indeed, can also help against this effect, but it seems that only works for the bearer, and not anyone else in the party.

The only other effect that this stone has is to make it difficult to foretell any events that take place within the fortress walls. This seems to stem from the fact that it blocks the magical energy needed to do so."

Asvartha finished reading, and closed the book. She thought about what to do next. With this knowledge, they knew it wouldn't be easy, but there was still hope if the objects were still able to be used against the dark dragon.

"What do you think, Your Highness?" asked the knight, after allowing her some time to ponder. "Should we go back to the capital to prepare, or should we go straight to the lair with the weapons?"

"Before we do anything else, let's get out of this cramped lab." The four dragons followed her lead, and untied their horses as soon as they reached them.

Before they could head off, however, they heard a screeching, and Horzkar's hawk flew in with a message on his leg, and landed on his master's wrist. The water realm's king had gotten their message when they had sent it from the earth realm, and let them know when they got there that he had sent it on with another message to the queen of Rhodran.

Indeed, it was a message from that very queen to them that the hawk was carrying, and the princess soon had it opened and began to read the familiar writing.

"I have been informed that you all have arrived back in the realm to find the magical weapons and

complete your quest. I wish you all luck, and am afraid that I can relay no updated news to you, at least as of yet. I have received everything that was sent to me, and shall take good care of your pet while you are gone, daughter.

You may tell Horzkar that his hawk has been a most excellent messenger for me. So much so that I shall have to compensate him for his hawk's services when you all return."

After quickly writing out a response to the queen to tell her that they had acquired what they sought and would head immediately to the fire realm and the dark dragon's lair, the silver princess bemusedly thought to herself that they would have plenty to tell her about their journey when they returned.

The hawk was sent off, and as they watched him

disappear off in the direction of the capital, they gave the command to their horses and started off. Nonetheless, they couldn't help but wonder what they were riding into. The end of all this, one way or another, but still they couldn't just do nothing. They had what they came for, and now was the time to strike.

CHAPTER TWELVE

As the small band began their journey to the lair of the dark dragon to settle things with him once and for all, now with the gauntlet and spear in their arsenal, their spirits were running high. They knew that at this point, the dark dragon would likely know what they were up to, but with the weapons in their grasp, they would be able to even the odds, especially against creatures of dark magic.

Even their horses seemed to have caught the spirit and were carrying them along a little bit faster than usual. Their exuberance was somewhat tempered, however, when they realized just how far the dark dragon had encroached on the world that they had known.

The trip through Rhodran went somewhat smoothly. They had stayed or camped where necessary when they or their horses needed to rest. It was a different story once they reached the borders of the fire kingdom.

The princess couldn't help remembering what they had overheard in a tavern they had stopped at last night.

"Did you hear yet?" they heard one tavern patron discussing what seemed to be the latest news with another, "about the fire realm? The king held out for as long as he could, and did a fine job of keeping Laubadar busy. They say he was captured last night, though. Locked in the dark dragon's dungeon with the other two captured kings. It seems Laubadar will likely be after the earth kingdom next, he doesn't like water too much, they say, so he's likely saving the water realm for last."

With the fire realm now occupied, it will be much harder to progress to the lair now, the princess mused.

She sighed. *But we have to find our way into the lair, by hook or by crook. Otherwise this will never end, except with Laubadar winning, and that's not an option.*

The five dragons had all taken the time, before they left the tavern, to put on their fire realm cloaks, and to put on the scent dampening potion they had been given. It likely wouldn't fool Laubadar's forces of lichs for long, but every effort to buy themselves as much time as possible was worth it.

The band crossed over the border as quickly as possible, expecting that there might be sentries posted to inspect anyone coming in, but it seemed that Laubadar had not sent them yet, or else didn't think he needed to, as there seemed to be no other living beings around for miles.

They could tell when they crossed, almost immediately. The terrain changed from more grassy, to very rocky and rough. The fire realm was naturally so, although it seemed that, somehow, since Laubadar was now in charge, that the extremely hard and sharp volcanic obsidian rocks that were rarer in this realm under normal circumstances now appeared to be more common. Come to think of it, the ice and snow in the ice dragon realm had also been worse than would normally be expected. Could Laubadar actually be changing the landscape? Was this a result of his seizing power from the rulers, or his dark magic? Or was it all just coincidence?

She remembered the text and how the lair had been chosen for its special attributes. Did that extend to the realm that had been chosen as well? It certainly sounded like something Laubadar would do, he seemed to have long term goals the first time he tried to take over the realms.

Soon, though, the party realized the reason why he hadn't bothered to post guards: the shadow-lichs appeared around them from their smoky mist, and it quickly became a fight to escape. They were soon tangled in a scratching, biting, bucking and rearing mass of shadow-lichs, and furiously trying to get them to draw back to even have room to breathe.

"Well, I guess he knows we're here now." the

dragon knight quipped, hacking and slashing with his sword, to which the mage had added some spells to make it more effective against the lichs, as she had with all their weapons.

"Listen everyone!" Asvartha called, "If we can break through their ranks, we might be able to run and shake them off."

The silver dragon took the lead and gave the example, she attacked one group of lichs head on, hoping to cause the line to break and make an opening. The mage finally made the opening they needed by blasting a few of them and knocking them away. The remainder tried to close the gap, but the dragons managed to get through before they could.

The lichs gave chase, of course. The horses were fortunately just fast enough to keep ahead of them, but the beasts were still nipping at the horses' heels.

"This isn't going to work unless we can lose them." the scholar, who had taken the rear of the line, called to the others.

Suddenly, the lich who was following him swiped at the feet of the scholar's horse, and it stumbled. The knight, who was the closest, turned his horse as quick as lightning and was hacking and slashing to keep the lichs off of the scholar and his horse.

The others turned around quickly to assist; by this time, the scholar had been able to remount his horse, and was swinging his staff to drive them back.

The other three, who were outside the circle of lichs, decided to help by attacking from the outside while the others attacked from the inside.

After the mage and the rogue rushed over to join in the melee, the princess made her decision. She hadn't wanted to use their secret weapon this early, but she might as well get some practice in. Besides, the gauntlet and spear were specifically designed to counteract dark magic, and these shadow-lichs were nothing if not dark magic.

There was another reason beyond that, though. Their only other option out of this situation would be to have the mage use the teleport spell again. That would drain her seriously, and put her out of commission for the final battle. They couldn't risk that. Also, they had already taken a pretty serious beating from these lichs, and they would need her healing powers at full strength to recover.

She drew out the gauntlet and spear, and slid the gauntlet on her right hand. She took the spear in her right hand, too.

She raised it, and began riding around the ring of lichs, stabbing here and there at them. She was amazed at how effective the spear seemed to be when activated. She seemed to barely need to touch them with the tip of the spear, and they just melted away, back into the insubstantial shadows and smoke from whence they came.

With Asvartha dealing with the lichs, and some of them already taken care of, the line broke easily, and the group finished them off.

"So what now? Did that take care of them?" the knight asked.

"More than likely not." the mage answered him. "They'll be back, just like last time with my spells, though not for a while until they've regenerated. In the meantime, it's up to us to hightail it out of here and get to a hiding spot. These skirmishes have tired us out, too, and our horses. We need to find a place to safely rest before we continue on to the lair."

The princess, meanwhile had been putting away the spear and gauntlet, and after doing so, led them, at a slower pace now, so as to not tire the horses further, towards the forest. There they found a cave, not far off the trail, large enough for them and their horses. The exhausted dragons lit a fire and laid out their sleeping pads.

The mage went to work putting protective spells and barriers up to prevent anyone else from entering the cave. She also took care of the many scratches, wounds, and scrapes on both them and their horses. In her long periods of study, she had not neglected to also study up on the healing arts, and could mend many injuries almost instantly. She also used the healing potions she had brought along for some of their injuries. The lichs may have been defeated for now, but they had made sure to leave their mark nonetheless. If the group was going to continue on to their final battle, they needed to be in top shape, and injuries from this battle could not be left to cause trouble later.

They also used the time to discuss their plans. If there was one thing one did not want to do when it came to the dark dragon, it was rush off without a plan.

"So," said the knight, who was beginning to feel better since the mage had finished healing his wounds, "you start a plan by determining your goal. Why are you going into that fortress? What is the ultimate objective? Well, that's easy: to reach the throne room and confront the dark dragon. Now, achieving that objective, especially in this case, is going to be easier said than done. You're either going to need a long series of distractions, some disguise, or sheer luck that would be almost impossible to imagine."

"The next question you ask yourself," he continued, "is what do you already know, and what can you imply from it? Well, we know now that he has finally taken, pretty much, the fire realm, and so is probably going to be able to boost his forces here. The result? It's going to be harder for us to get in there. That leaves us with only a couple of options: The teleport spell and covert operations. Since the teleport spell is off the table, that leaves us with only one choice. I suggest that we stop and go stealth mode when we near the fortress. I can go ahead alone, on foot, and you four stay back. I will go around the back of the fortress, and try to knock out some guards to get us some clothes or armor. Once we have that, we'll be set. It might be possible to go all the way to the throne room doors that way."

"I might be able to assist you with that, too." added the mage. "Your scouting would definitely be assisted by my stealth and invisibility spells."

"Okay," the princess interjected, "that will get us in, but how can we win the battle against Laubadar himself?"

"When we finally do get to that fight," he responded, "we'll need to do what the book said: use our powers in tandem to maximum effect. We'll hit him with everything we've got, all at once. If that doesn't work, then we fall back on attack and retreat, one or two of us at a time, the rest of us out of range, and hope to wear him down. If you can keep out of the way of his offensive spells and physical attacks long enough, no one can keep going forever. He may seem more powerful, but power doesn't count for much if you can't hit your target."

The next morning, just before sunrise, they packed up and left the cave to start back on their way. It didn't take long before they saw a group of sentries coming up the road.

"Should we confront them?" asked the dragon knight.

"Perhaps with our garb, they won't recognize us and will let us pass." the mage said.

However, the sentries had been sent out because the lichs were reforming themselves, and had orders to search everyone.

Because of that, the five dragons were forced to

confront them, and after a small battle, they tried to figure out what to do with their unconscious foes.

The mage and the princess agreed that they should switch their garb for the guard's armor, so that they might fit in better, should they come across any more scouts. They also needed some way to get in, and blending in and being allowed entrance to the lair would be much easier than having to fight their way in. Even the king of the fire realm had been unable to hold against the lair of Laubadar.

They put the sentries on the back of their horses and took their armor off, replacing it with their cloaks, and decided they would walk in the armor with the sentries on their horses. They had them tied and gagged, and they were still out cold.

As the knight had been struck by the sword of one

of the sentries, the mage took time to heal him before they left, as they were putting on the sentry's armor.

With that taken care of, they hurried on their way, now that their horses were refreshed, and with the armor, they didn't have any more trouble with the sentries on the roads. It was evident that Laubadar was desperate to catch them, as they seemed to come upon a new group at fairly regular intervals as they went along.

It wasn't long before they could see their destination in the distance. For them, in a lot of ways, it was a relief, as it meant that, with any luck, their troubles would soon be over. However, they also knew that Laubadar didn't go down without a fight for the royal mage, and was unlikely to do so now.

The group, still in their disguises, came up on the

gates to the lair. Since the knight was the one with the most thorough understanding of protocol, they left it to him to get them past the gates. He managed to convince the guards that they were fellow sentries, delivering prisoners to the fortress, and they soon found themselves inside its walls.

This fortress was undoubtedly unlike any of the others the five dragons had ever seen. The entire place, from bottom to top, seemed to be a gigantic mountain of obsidian rock, with the sides sheer and imposing, with every pointed turret a seemingly natural extension of the points of the mountain, with some of them even being difficult to tell if it was one or the other.

The sun would have reflected brightly off of the black stone, if the sun had been out that day. It didn't take the reflection, though, to tell that the entire surface of the mountain, and thus the castle that was carved from it, had a natural sheen and polish. One couldn't help but think that it might even have been beautiful, in its own way, if it only had another owner to improve the atmosphere of the place.

Once inside, the five young dragons put their horses in stalls in the stables, and the sentries, still unconscious and tied up, in another. They followed a group of guards to a back door that seemed to be reserved for the fortress' guards to come and go, and entered into the main part of the fortress.

Just as from the outside, the rooms and passageways here were also carved from the very mountain itself, and the darkness was only increased by the dark stone that the walls were carved out of. The torches that were placed along the walls seemed to do nothing to change this, as if the very mood and fabric of the fortress was fouled by the dark arts of its master.

They slipped away from the other group, into a seemingly empty room. When they looked around, it seemed to be a map room of sorts, because they found maps of the other realms, and a map with the layout of the fortress as well. Rordgur took some time to study it, and found where the throne room was.

"Here, all the way on the other side, to the front of the fortress, near the front foyer area, that's the throne room; probably where he'll be waiting." the scholar told the others, pointing to the map.

"Where are the dungeons?" asked the princess.

"Here." the blue dragon pointed again. "Usually those go underground, but these are pretty high up in the mountain. I guess they couldn't dig down through this hard rock, or else they wanted the prisoners to be high up to discourage escape. We can go there and free everyone as soon as we deal with the dark dragon."

The knight peeped his head out, and when he signaled it was clear, they all followed him out, and began to head towards the throne room. There was no need to waste time, Laubadar's forces would fall apart once he was taken care of.

The group, now more determined than ever, followed the knight as he led them down the smooth, dark stone lined hallways. There were few sounds, except the random passing of a group of chattering guards or servants.

After what seemed like an eternity, they made it to the front foyer. Just as they were passing through, though, one of the lichs on guard there must have sensed that they weren't guards, and jumped on the knight and knocked him over, pinning him down and knocking off his helmet. It roared in his face, and then turned and let out a piercing screech, seemingly to call its fellows for assistance.

"Well, I guess that blows our cover, but that's actually okay with me." Eordwar said, as he tossed off his helmet and drew out his dagger to prepare to assist the knight. The others followed suit. They still kept on the breastplates, though, as those still afforded some protection, if not disguise any longer.

The rest of the group reached the knight as the rogue had already gotten there and started slashing at the beast. Some more were coming, by the sounds of the thumping and screeching they could hear down the hallways; the backup for this one was already on its way.

A horde of shadow-lichs and dragon-lichs reached

the entrance and started to come into the foyer room. Targarma was using her magic to charge her wand and then began spinning around to send blasts out all around to keep the shadow-lichs at bay. The rogue was using his skills at knife throwing that he had perfected in his trial to hit them from long range.

The mage fired off her most powerful light based spell. The room lit up with an almost blinding light. When it died down, the shadow-lichs had all dissipated into smoke, or retreated.

However, they hadn't time to even catch their breath, because the sentries were already coming into the foyer, having heard the commotion just as much as the shadow-lichs had.

The second-in-command of the dark dragon had also come, unfortunately for his five opponents.

"Get them! They may have gotten past the shadow-lichs, but don't let them get any further! Show the dark dragon your loyalty!" he called to the sentries.

The dragons didn't want to have to use lethal force against living beings, but were prepared to, if necessary.

They aimed only to knock them unconscious, if possible. The mage fired stunning spells, which turned out to be fairly effective, and as for the rest of the group; the scholar used sweeps with his staff, or blows to the head, and the knight sent a fair few crumpling to the ground with his mace to their head, which would have been worse for them if they hadn't been wearing their helmets. The princess and the rogue aimed their fists and daggers at places that would take their foes down without killing them.

The group took down the last of the sentries, just

like the lichs before, and turned to the sound of the second-in-command's voice when he began speaking.

"I'll give you this; you're extremely lucky. However, your luck has just run out, because I'll handle you all myself."

He came forward to face the group, and the knight strode towards him.

"You, take on all of us? One on five? No, that's not necessary. I'm all that's needed to deal with you. I did before, and I will again."

The two of them circled, squaring off against each other. With a mighty battle cry, the two rushed at each other. The knight got first draw, and very nearly got a hit in on the lieutenant's shoulder before he could counter, just missing him by a mere hair's breadth.

However, they could tell by the way that the second-in-command kept nearly step for step with their knight that this wasn't going to be easy. It hadn't been last time, and with that likely driving his foe, the knight had to watch himself.

Arkdhar once almost backed Horzkar up against a wall when he knocked his sword from his hand. The knight, though, had been trained in what to do when empty-handed, and managed to dodge the blow, roll and grab his sword, and get back in the battle.

The dark dragon's second-in-command was far from down, though. He seemed to be remembering that defeat, and was fairly determined that it wouldn't happen again.

The two combatants parried and dueled all around the room, one sometimes gaining the upper hand, sometimes the other. The sounds of clashing steel and the panting of the two tiring dragons were the only sounds to be heard.

Horzkar only just managed to avoid a blow that sliced the helmet off of one of the suits of armor along the wall, and from then on, he kept a greater distance from his opponent, unless he was darting in for an opening.

Finally it seemed his opponent was tiring enough that he was leaving big openings in his defenses. The dragon knight took full advantage of this, slicing with his sword at every opportunity that presented itself.

As if in agreement that they should finish the duel, the two of them, having spaced themselves out, stood still for a moment, almost as if sizing their opponent up for one last strike. They were both alert for the slightest twitch that signified movement from their opponent. The two of them, still staring, leaped towards each other within a split second.

The mace of the dragon knight, which he was now using since he had gotten his sword stuck in the wall on an attempt to strike his foe, hit its mark. The second-in-command's sword hit its mark, as well, but thanks to hitting the breastplate, didn't go as deep as he was aiming for. The mace connected, and sent the dragon flying across the room into the wall with its force.

After the battle that the knight had, they knew he would need time to catch his breath. His opponent, still out cold, lay slumped against the wall and was not likely to be going anywhere in a hurry either, even once he came to.

Every one of them knew, though, that by this time

the element of surprise would be totally lost. There would be no way that Laubadar didn't hear that battle, or even the ones before it. They would have to hurry, or else he might even have a trap set, that is, if he didn't already. He more than likely had, or else he would have probably already come to deal with them himself.

Once the knight had a good chance to catch his breath and recover his sword, they all rushed down the hallway, now devoid of guards, seeing as they had all likely come running to the source of the noise, the battle in the foyer, and been knocked out, injured or both in the conflict. They came to a stop in front of the doors at the end of the corridor.

They found themselves standing in front of two huge, detailed, and jet black doors, made out of the darkest mahogany that any of them had ever seen. It would probably take all of them to push them open.

The five dragons all looked at each other for a moment before going to open the doors. This was the final battle, with everything at stake. The dragon knight, now feeling back to normal, and ready to go again, gave the princess and the others a thumbs up. They all moved as one, and began pushing open the doors to the dark dragon's throne room.

CHAPTER THIRTEEN

As the five dragons entered the now open doors to complete what they'd come here to do, they quickly looked around for their target. The mage muttered an incantation under her breath to provide a barrier for some assurance against anyone intruding on their battles. No one else could enter the room until this was all over.

The dark dragon was indeed in the throne room, sitting pompously on his throne, his tail swishing. He had caught sight of them as well. They hadn't expected him to be so large, his bulk took up a good portion of that area of the room. He was a stark reminder of the majesty of the ancient dragons. His magic had warped him into a form more akin to those great forbears. While most dragons normally had two horns, or none, he had four, and the second pair was like a ram's which curled downwards in a spiral. His back and tail were lined with spikes that ran all down his spine, all likely effects of the dark magic he practiced.

The throne itself was different from the rest of the palace. True, it too was carved out of jet black obsidian, but all in one piece out of a separate block from the rest of the fortress, and had silver fittings on the feet, which formed claws, the arms, and the tips of the back of the chair had round, silver spheres attached. Little silver figures of dragons stood on top of the spheres. The back was carved in relief with a giant, black dragon, breathing fire.

The large dragon let out a deep, rumbling, ominous chuckle at the sight of them.

"Five? They send so few against me? I had heard, of course, that there was a group who sought to find the objects to stop me, but I thought perhaps they'd have been wise enough to send more than five. I almost pity you. However, it simply makes it all the more easy to show them what a mistake it is to underestimate me so."

"You might not think so little of us, perhaps, once the battle starts," the knight retorted.

The great dark dragon raised himself up off of his throne, and rushed at them at full tilt; all five of the dragons took their stances and braced for the impact. The mage's reflexes were just as quick as her opponent's, though, and she had put up a barrier just in time. Laubadar struck the barrier, and it resisted him. The knight's reflexes proved nearly as good, he had already drawn his sword and mace in case the mage hadn't been able to get the barrier up in time.

"Remember the plan," the knight said in a low voice, "when he breaks through, be ready and attack all at once."

The princess brought out the spear and gauntlet. This did not go unnoticed by Laubadar. It only seemed to increase his frenzy. He smashed through the barrier, and in a lightning quick instant, before the princess could get the gauntlet on, had knocked them, and almost her, to the other side of the room. They came to rest near the back of the room, right beside his throne.

"Don't be thinking you'll be getting off that easy; I

don't intend to give you the chance to use those, not this time." the dark dragon snarled.

The princess drew her dagger, still intending to fight that way for as long as she could, and then, when an opening arose, to make for the back of the room to collect the objects. It was clear, though, that they were going to have to nearly completely wear him down before there would be a chance to use them.

The distraction, though, had at least allowed the others to attack. The knight was hacking away, although Laubadar was himself good with barrier spells, so most of his blows weren't landing. The mage was trying to use counter-spells to disarm his barrier, but that would take time. The rogue was also working hard to find an opening, and the scholar was attempting to strike tripping blows to the black dragon's legs with his staff.

Their opponent, meanwhile, was of course not taking this lying down. He attempted to land blows, but fortunately, many of his failed to land as well. The scholar parried his kicks and blows with his staff, and the knight and rogue were swift enough to retreat out of his strike range for a time if a blow failed to connect.

The rogue took a huge jump, assisted by his wings, and managed to land on the dark dragon's head and grab hold of his horns. He was hoping to perhaps get him to smack into the wall, or else pull him down, but the larger dragon was having none of it. With a bellowing roar, he reared up and shook the rogue off, sending him smacking into a side wall.

The mage, who had been chanting her incantations all the while, finally managed to break Laubadar's barrier, which he had just put up again. The knight and rogue darted in to attack, landing a few blows, as did the scholar. The mage fired off a few volleys of magic blasts, and the princess also made a few hits. They knew, though, that they were going to have to try something different, because trying to take him down with a few lucky hits each time his barrier went down was only going to wear them out first.

Laubadar was quickly back on the offensive, though, and tried another charge attack. Once again, the mage's barrier protected them. The knight said it was time to switch tactics, just as they had planned, and begin to use their elemental abilities to the full.

"Remember," he said, "don't hold anything back. Rordgur, you're with me, we're up first."

The blue scholar dragon nodded, and stepped forward with the knight. Their foe once again tried to charge, but instead of bracing themselves, they prepared to use their abilities.

The blue dragon summoned his ice abilities, and aimed at the dark dragon's feet. Almost in an instant, the dragon literally froze in his tracks, his feet encumbered in chunks of ice. The scholar didn't stop there, however, he covered most of the floor in a sheet of ice as well.

"They were right about that dampening effect on dragon's abilities," the scholar mused. "If that had been at full power, this whole room, floor to ceiling, would have been covered in ice. I bet it has something to do with keeping the prisoners from escaping."

Meanwhile, they had darted in to land some blows on the dark dragon, who all the while was thrashing about. They still had to avoid his tail, as it could have easily sent them flying.

With a mighty, resounding crack, the huge beast shivered the ice to pieces, and the two slid back out of range of his attacks.

Laubadar, however, was not so agile on the ice. He could barely move a few inches forward, without beginning to lose his balance and slip on the ice. His two opponents decided to use this to their advantage. They saw that this had slowed him down, so they took up positions just in front of and in back of him.

Whenever the great dark dragon tried to attack either one of them, the other would dart in and strike, diverting his attention back to them. If the dark dragon made too jerky of a movement towards this new distraction, he would slide on the ice. They had to avoid his blasts of flame breath, but managed to just keep out of its range.

After they had distracted his attention in this manner a few times, the scholar quickly climbed one of the pillars that lined the walls of the throne room; and while the knight kept their enemy focused on him, the blue dragon jumped on Laubadar's head, just as the rogue had done.

This time, however, the force of his momentum caused the black dragon to slide, and they struck the far wall. The blue dragon jumped off just before they hit.

The dark dragon shook himself and stood up. He had to have taken damage, as the impact had left a large dent in the wall. The knight and the scholar had retreated back a ways, and Laubadar, now very angry, charged against them, but was hindered once again by the ice. He turned his anger towards that now, and let loose a giant blast of flame that melted it. The mage had to put a barrier around the two to keep them from being caught in the flames.

It was the first time that anyone had ever really been able to land such a blow against the dark dragon. It raised the group's hopes, and they saw that their foe was indeed not unbeatable. It could mean things were turning around for them.

Their foe had stopped his assault, and was apparently prepping for another charge at them, when the knight leapt in again.

"Now, it's my turn!" Horzkar called out, landing a volley of blows, hacks, and slashes, as well as bursts of his fire breath against the enemy, fulfilling his job to keep him distracted while the scholar refroze the ice on the floor from the water that Laubadar's breath had melted it into.

It would seem, though, that the dark dragon was

not to be taken by the same tricks twice. With several great pounds of his feet, accompanied by resounding thuds, quite a bit of the ice around him was cracked, rendering it easier for him to move again. He followed this by trying to attack them with dark magic, but found the collars they were wearing just as effective against him as those worn by his royal prisoners.

In his rage, he whipped around his tail, which struck the two and sent them flying into the walls, and quickly followed that up by once again releasing a massive blast of fire breath to melt the ice he hadn't smashed. The mage had to quickly levitate the two unconscious members of their team over to them, and put up the barrier again to defend against the flames.

Since the mage and the rogue had now recuperated somewhat from the earlier battle, they were ready to take their turn against the dark dragon.

That very same dragon was now finally letting off with the fire breath enough that they could maneuver themselves.

"Ready to go?" asked the mage, turning to Eordwar.

"Always ready" came the reply.

The two new combatants stepped up, and, with weapons drawn, faced the foe. This time the dark dragon tried rearing up, and ended up smashing into Targarma's barrier. The barrier broke this time, but the two had just enough time to roll out of the way. Fortunately it took just as little time for the mage to disarm Laubadar's barrier this time, and they dealt blows and fired spells as quickly as they could before they had to retreat out of the danger zone.

The mage was a specialist with water elemental

abilities, and the water that Laubadar had melted gave her an idea.

"Use your elemental abilities." she said to the rogue, just as they had to split in different directions due to Laubadar's massive tail slamming down between them.

While the mage caught their pursuer's attention with a blast from her staff, the green dragon prepared to use his abilities, which for earth dragons, manifested not only as control of plants and their growth, but geomancy as well.

The ground began to rumble and shake, almost as if it were an earthquake, but then several boulders started to burst through the floor, standing almost pillar-like across the room, although not in any defined pattern.

The mage and the rogue leaped on top of the stones that now littered the area. The princess, who was observing the battle and looking after the other two dragons, who were beginning to come to, thought she saw their plan.

This is good, it could definitely work. Not only does it make it easier to get around over the slippery water on the floor from Laubadar melting the ice, but it makes it harder for him to move around, being so large. That will make him much slower, and a much easier target than he has been so far.

The two had a more intricate plan than that, though. They continuously leaped from stone to stone to avoid the larger dragon, while darting in for a strike, or, in the case of the mage, using her powers long range, even firing off multiple blasts, all while deftly avoiding the enraged would-be king's slashes, tail-whips, and snaps.

Eventually their enemy became so enraged that he began smashing into the rocks, butting them with his head, and slamming them with his tail. They were reduced to dirt clods, and mixed with the water still left on the floor.

This was what the two of them had been waiting for. Eordwar once again used his geomancy, however, this time, he used it on the thick mud that now stood at all of their feet. The dark dragon didn't notice the mud, directed by the green dragon, creeping up his legs and hardening until it stopped him in his tracks.

He once again began to struggle, just as he had with the ice, but the two were closing the gap once more to get in another barrage while the dragon was held fast by his bonds. He was having a harder time to escape the mud than he had the ice, and even he knew that his fire breath wouldn't help him in this situation as it had in that one.

The voice of the knight caused the princess to turn back in that direction. He was awake again, now, and so was the scholar. She nodded to them, motioning with her head towards the throne, and they nodded back, understanding.

She took off, keeping to the shadows near the walls, hoping this would help to conceal her, although the dark dragon was very tied up, what with fending off his opponents and all, and they certainly weren't letting up. The knight and the scholar were ready to step back in if they had to, but if she were quick enough, they might not even have to do that.

She made her way along the walls, pausing to see if

she had been spotted. Laubadar was having an unusually hard time with the mud, which was allowing the mage and the rogue to keep him well distracted and focused on them.

The silver princess finally reached the throne, and there beside it lay the two magical weapons that they had all worked so hard to get. She scooped them up and quickly put on the gauntlet and in her right hand, on which she was wearing it, she grasped the spear. It opened up to its full height, almost as tall as her.

Immediately upon the activation of the gauntlet and spear, the dragoness could tell that a strong force field barrier sparked to life across the doorway, even stronger than the protection spells and barriers that their mage had put up when they entered.

The lichs that served Laubadar had by this time

reformed themselves, and were trying to get in, but couldn't get past the barrier, despite their best efforts. This battle was between those already in the room now.

The battle between the rogue, the mage, and their foe carried on, with the dark dragon making one mighty effort to break free of the mud that the earth dragon had hardened all around them, looking for all the world as if it were just the ground outside. The result of his efforts to break free were that he finally got loose, sending dirt flying in every direction, and that the force knocked the two other combatants into the wall.

All this time, he had been distracted by his struggles, but the dark dragon almost immediately noticed that the princess was no longer with the group. He wheeled around, and saw that she was standing by the throne, and had the objects.

This was what she had been waiting for, and she tensed as she waited for him to make the first move. He wasted no time, and immediately charged at her again. She knew the mage's spells wouldn't help her now that Targarma was unconscious, but neither perhaps, did she need them now.

The princess thought quickly and took to the air with her wings, using them to propel her through the air, barely dodging a swipe of the furious dragon's tail, which hit the wall and left nothing but a pile of rubble and a hole in the wall behind it. She had to use the gauntlet's blast of energy against some of the debris that was flying to keep it from hitting her, but she managed to fly past unscathed.

She glided downwards, having reached the other side of the room, and landed, skidding to a stop, near her group. The knight and scholar had rushed over as soon as Laubadar's attention fell on the princess, and were looking after the other two.

Their foe, meanwhile, had also stopped his charge and turned around, facing their direction once more, and looking as if he were preparing for another charge.

Asvartha knew that the rest of this battle would be hers and hers alone. The others had done their part, and she was grateful to them; now it was time to finish what they had started.

The dark dragon, however, seemed to be changing tactics in the battle at this point. Rather to say, he dropped any semblance of tactics, and simply fought like a cornered wild animal that knows the hunter is near. He was driven now only by the fact that he recognized that his fate was drawing in on him, and that he was very unlikely to be able to escape it now. His foes had the one thing that could bring his plans to a halt, and it was driving him mad.

The eye could barely keep up with him, as he snapped, stomped, and thrashed about, swinging his tail; he obviously hoped to keep the princess too busy dodging him and his attacks to use the weapons against him. Despite his bulk, he was quite quick, and surprisingly agile as well. However, he was nowhere near the level of the speed that came with being smaller and much less heavily built. This allowed the princess to gracefully leap around to avoid all his strikes.

He began to swing his tail hard, hoping to land a crushing blow, but she avoided the battering ram with the aid of some gliding leaps with the use of her wings. Once, he even swung hard enough to cave the wall and part of the ceiling down on them both. The other four held their breaths, waiting to see any sign of movement.

The princess pushed aside some rubble, having held the gauntlet above her head to take most of the blow from the rubble and to prevent her from being knocked out by the falling debris.

Moments later, the dark dragon too was seen to emerge from the pile of stones, and they once more took up their positions to resume the fight.

She stepped out into the room, facing her enemy directly, and took her stance.

"Laubadar, this ends today," she shouted. "your control over these realms, your attempts to gain power, and your threats to the peace, are all over. You are going to return to your prison, and become nothing more than what you were before, a distant memory."

In response, the huge black dragon roared, loud enough to make the ceiling rumble, lowered his head and charged.

The dragoness raised the spear, aimed, and threw. The spear flew through the air, and, unable to stop his forward momentum, the dark dragon couldn't dodge it. It hit its mark square in the chest, and immediately the webs of the crystal prison that had held him before reformed to enclose him again. Soon, just as before, the crystal shrank, with the dark dragon inside, and hung there for a moment before falling to the ground.

The victor came and picked up the crystal. She saw that, just as it had been described before, it looked like any ordinary crystal, with the exception of a swirling, shadowy mass in the center, in the shape of a dragon.

The lichs had dissolved back into the shadows,

fading out of existence along with their master. They would trouble the realms no more, any more than the dark dragon. Those that had been transformed to dragon-lichs were returned to normal, just as before.

By the time the princess returned to the rest of her group, she was relieved to see that Targarma and Eordwar were beginning to come to. They had been tended by the knight and the scholar, and were soon sitting up.

"So, it looks like it's over." Eordwar commented.

"Yes, finally," the princess replied, showing them the crystal. "I have to thank you all for this victory, you put a lot on the line, and I would never have been able to wear him down enough without you."

"We simply did our part, as required. We weren't about to let him win," the dragon knight replied, pointing to the crystal containing Laubadar.

"There will be much to do now," said the mage, "for everyone in all the realms, but at least the realms can heal once more, and eventually return to peace."

They were beginning to hear the stirrings of the sentries, and, soon, with some of them having come to see that they were too late to prevent their master's overthrow, some began shuffling out of the gates, while others still talked of trying to avenge him, although practically they knew that if these dragons had defeated the dark dragon, they would have no chance, and so hesitated to be the first ones to make a move towards revenge.

"So, the lichs are gone," said the rogue, "but what do we do with these guys?" He pointed to the gathering of the sentries that had now all come to from their earlier battle.

"Our first priority," replied the princess, "will be to release Laubadar's captives. The kings can decide what to do with these followers afterwards."

For the most part, the crowd parted to allow them to pass when the mage dropped the magical barrier. The knight moved in the lead in case there were any challenges, but the mage's force field bubble also helped to ensure that they were left undisturbed.

They received the keys from a guard who handed them over without protest, and proceeded to the cells. They immediately began checking each one. The empty ones were left unlocked, they found. Whenever they came upon one that was locked, they unlocked it to release the prisoner.

One of the first of these that they came across was

the cell of Karvarthuk, the sovereign of the ice dragon realm.

Once they had confirmed a prisoner was in a cell, the princess would enter to release them from their shackles. The dragon king thanked her profusely, then informed them that he would head downstairs to oversee the detaining of the guards who were the dark dragon's followers.

The small victorious group continued on, releasing every prisoner they came across, and eventually came to the cell containing the king of Rhodran.

"Father!" the princess called out when she saw him through the bars in the cell door. "Hang on, we're coming."

She soon had the door open and the shackles undone. The two, more than overjoyed at seeing each other, shared a tight embrace, the first in many months. Neither of them seemed particularly in a hurry to release it, and wordlessly shared how happy they both were to catch their first sight of each other in a long time.

CHAPTER FOURTEEN

The other four Rhodran dragons stayed back to allow the princess to have time with her father, and watched as they caught up on their missing time.

"I'll keep moving through the cells and releasing the other prisoners," the knight said, and they heard the door creak as he left.

"So," Valwardus said, as soon as they were finished hugging, "I can only assume that as you all are here releasing all the prisoners, you must have succeeded in defeating the dark dragon?"

In response, Asvartha showed him the crystal, once again containing the treacherous dragon.

Its red glow was lighter now than the king had seen it before. He figured it must be the stronger the spell was, as it would be when fresh, it suppressed the powers of whatever it held, in order to keep it trapped inside. It must have been glowing so brightly when they had first seen it as a warning that the spell was about to break entirely.

Other than that, it looked the same. The swirling mass of black energy inside, that represented Laubadar's essence, was more turbulent than he had seen it before. He was trying, and failing, to weaken his new prison.

"That's nothing short of amazing for ones so young.

I knew the council would make the right choices as to who to send with you. You have to tell me all about what happened."

The princess sat down and talked for a long time. She told her father all they had seen and experienced, all they had learned on their lengthy journey. As she spoke, she herself could barely believe all that they had done in their search, and that they had actually managed to succeed.

When she had finished, her father spoke again, turning to the other three dragons that remained in the room.

"I really can't thank you enough for your assistance, and ensuring my daughter's safety. I know that this couldn't have been an easy mission to complete for any of you."

"Thank you, Your Majesty," said the mage, speaking for all of them, "but we chose to do so freely, because of the very fact that we knew what the stakes were if we had refused."

Just then, the knight came back from having freed the other prisoners, and he entered with the fire realm's king, who wanted to speak with King Valwardus.

"What's the latest news?" the king of Rhodran asked his fellow king. "What do we do now that Laubadar's forces are broken up?"

"That's exactly what I was intending to talk about. We need to come up with a plan to keep this from happening again, from the bottom up. Karvarthuk has already taken charge here, and is already rounding up the sentries under Laubadar's service in the square outside to decide their fate. The ones that refuse to take oaths of loyalty to the realms will have to be imprisoned somewhere; there's no way we can just let them go free. Some of them are just now coming to from the earlier battles. I guess you five must have really done a number on them."

The fire realm's king turned to the five young heroes, who he could see were smirking at his comment.

"I think we may as well make use of this place, it no doubt has plenty of dungeons." Valwardus reasoned. "We could arrange to have a contingent of guards from all of the realms to take shifts to guard the ones who refuse to renounce their loyalty to Laubadar."

"That could work. It seems that Laubadar didn't keep too many sentries; he apparently preferred his lichs. Easier to fully control, I guess." the fire king agreed.

The princess added, "We've also got to figure out what to do with the objects, and Laubadar's crystal. The way things were set up last time kept him at bay for quite a while, but how do we keep this from happening again?"

"I might have some ideas for that." the mage responded.

"And we would love to hear them and give them all due consideration," Valwardus said, standing up and stretching, "but first, let's get out of here and see how Karvarthuk is doing."

The entire group made their way out of the cell and down the long, dark corridor that held all the cells of the fortress. They proceeded down a winding staircase and out the ground floor corridor, all the while wondering why it was no brighter here in these halls than the one that held the dungeons.

When they reached the court outside through the great doors of the fortress, they saw that the ice kingdom's ruler had indeed been busy. He had quickly rallied his ice realm troops that had been taken here as captives, and now were released, to the end of keeping Laubadar's sentries in order and ensuring that they were dealt with. He had even taken temporary control of the fire realm forces that had been captured.

Karvarthuk already had everything in relative calm by the time they got there. They explained their idea to him, and he agreed. He had his men, who were patrolling the gathered crowd, get everyone's attention, and he laid out for the sentries what was going to happen.

"All of you," he began, "are currently enemies of the realms, for your loyalty to Laubadar. However, we are offering you a way to change that. We will be administering oaths of loyalty to the realms, beginning now, and those of you who take, and keep, that oath, will be granted pardons. Those who do not will be imprisoned here for lengths of time to be judged in the courts of the realms. We leave it to you, then, which of these to choose. Leave behind your allegiances and gain your freedom, or else face judgment for your part in the dark one's crimes."

As the ice realm monarch began that long process, with almost all of the former sentries choosing to take the oath, the king of Rhodran turned back to the mage to address another issue.

"So, what was your idea about what we should do with the crystal and the objects?"

"Well, Your Majesty, I'm not sure about the objects, but I hit upon an idea for the crystal that I think will keep it safe and hidden for a long time, perhaps permanently. Follow me."

The mage led them back into the fortress and straight to the throne room. She then led them to the massive hole that had been created as battle damage from Laubadar striking the wall with his tail.

"If you were to create a niche here, and place the crystal inside, and then seal up the wall with a covered entrance that would only open with strong magic, it might effectively hide the crystal for a long time."

Valwardus pondered this for a moment, and then said "Wouldn't a mage have to do that? Could you do it?"

"Most certainly, Your Majesty." the mage turned,

and began reciting the spell.

The hole in the wall began to gradually reform itself into a nook perfectly suited to holding something. It had a little raised area to place something on.

The princess brought out the crystal, and the mage encased it in a protective bubble of magic for further insurance against tampering.

Targarma then levitated the bubble with the crystal to the niche and released it to float there. She began intoning another spell and soon the rubble around them had repaired itself into a hidden, covered entrance, which when complete, hid the fact that anything was even there.

"Now," said the knight, "that just leaves what to do with the maps and the magical weapons. They need to be hidden again, too."

"Actually, I think the mage's idea has given me an idea about what to do with them." the princess smiled.

The fire realm king came in, and addressed Valwardus. "We've begun taking the oaths. Will you be staying, or are you going to leave soon?"

"I've been away from my kingdom for far too long. I'd like to head back as soon as possible."

"In that case," replied his fellow king, "we have a nice horse we saw in the stables we'd like to give to you."

"That reminds me," said the princess. "we forgot to tell you, your horses that you lent to us are in the stables as well. I know it took a long time to return them to you."

"Not a problem," chuckled the larger dragon. "In

fact, that's what I wanted to discuss with you. I think they're probably more yours than mine, now, and you all are the heroes of the realms, after all. They're yours. You can keep them."

"Thank you so much, Your Majesty."

The red dragon chuckled once again, and motioned to them to follow him to the stables. They could see that the ice realm king was a good organizer. He already had lines of former followers of Laubadar taking the oaths from his men. They passed this by and came to the stables.

The sight of their faithful horses, which had helped them through so much, endured wounds along with them, and been chased by the lichs while they were riding them, made them happier than ever.

The fire realm king led Valwardus to a beautiful

animal, coal black and with a long mane and tail, that had apparently been used by second-in-command of the dark dragon himself. It was slightly larger than the fire king's horses. Laubadar had been the one who actually owned the horse, but given his much larger size than a normal dragon, he preferred to get around solely on his massive wings; and allowed his second to use it.

"I can see why you were impressed. It's a magnificent animal." remarked the king of Rhodran, as he admired the mount.

They all led their saddled and bridled horses into the court, and mounted with the help of the fire realm's sovereign. They took their leave, and started off. The princess let them know that she had a stop along the way that she needed to make, related to her idea about what to do with the remaining weapons and maps, which she believed would ensure their safety.

They started off on their way, taking their time now, as they weren't being chased by the enemy or racing against a deadline. The very lands themselves seemed to be relieved of a burden, and the fire realm no longer seemed so gloomy as it had before.

It was certainly a nice change of pace, as they had been in such a rush before, that despite the fact that they had visited every other realm, which the princess had never done before, they had rushed through some of them so hurriedly that they didn't really even have much time to do or see much else but the trials before they had to move on elsewhere.

The travelers crossed the border between Teldros and Rhodran, and made their way back to the capital through the great forests. On the way, the princess led them slightly off the path to the location of the lab of Urdharmus.

"This is my plan. We re-hide the journal, maps, and the magical weapons here, but I'll need the mage's help. The rest of you can wait here for us."

The scholar nodded his head, he and the others agreeing to the plan, and took the journal and maps from his rucksack and handed them to the princess. She, in turn, drew out the gauntlet and spear from her luggage, and handed them to the mage to hold.

The two dragonesses dismounted, entering the passage to the lab once more. When they had almost reached the magic lab, they instead activated the hidden door to the passage that bypassed the lab and the trial passageway, and went straight through to the cavern that had held the gauntlet and spear.

The two items, they returned to their rightful place, and the princess asked for a few extra protections.

"Could you create another niche, to hide the journal and maps? Like you did to hide the crystal?"

"Certainly, Your Highness." the mage chanted the spell once more, and a small nook in the rocks of the wall appeared.

The journal and the maps were deposited in it, and the mage made a door, as she had with the crystal at the lair, and yet another to conceal the two magical weapons.

She then proceeded to also place protective barriers and seals on both hiding places, as an extra precaution, for only those, like them, who needed them to protect the realms, or for other good ends.

"That's it, then." the princess turned to her

companion. "The maps won't really be of any use anymore, but the journal's information will help whoever finds it here, along with the weapons, if they should happen to be needed again."

With their task now done, they made their way back out, and sealed the secret entrance as they left. With any luck, the chamber would remain undisturbed for a long time into the future; with an enormous amount of luck, maybe it would never have to be disturbed again.

They met back up with the rest of their party outside, mounted, and took off on their way again. It seemed like no time at all before they were coming up on the capital, and then the palace. The streets were full of crowds, cheering and greeting them, happy to see their king once again after several months now.

The group made their procession slowly, the king stopped to talk frequently, and mostly to reassure everyone who was thronging around that he would not be leaving the kingdom again anytime soon. The crowds also wanted to hear the story of the group of heroes, for the story had quickly spread far and wide about how they had defeated Laubadar in his very lair.

They had finally managed to wind through the streets to the palace, and the guards had let them in the gates, and the stable hands had led away their horses, when the queen came out to greet them. Not having seen either of them for some time, she was overjoyed to see them both back, and shared a long hug with each of them.

The others of the group were invited inside, and the king had it immediately announced that there would be a grand celebration for which everyone should come to the palace tomorrow night.

Shortly after nightfall the next day, all the townsfolk had gathered there to join the festivities. The king called for everyone's attention and began a speech.

"I started out on a journey, lifetimes ago now, it seems. I had a mission to protect my people, my realm, and all the other realms. I started with the hope that it would not be necessary to send this group of young dragons to finish the job, because I hoped to be able to do so myself. As it turns out, I was not, and instead, that burden was shouldered not only by my daughter, but these four other dragons you see here. They have done so admirably. Although I regret my inability to stop the dark dragon, I am forever grateful to all of them for their courage and strength."

"The dark dragon," he continued, "will trouble us no more. That is all to their credit. And so, I wish to present each of them with this realm's honors as a token of my gratitude."

The king, beckoning forth his chancellor, took from him a medal for each of the five dragons. The medals were made of gold, with blue ribbons, and a jewel in the middle of the pendant that matched the color of their scales. The king placed them around their necks, one at a time, as the crowd applauded.

When he got to his daughter, he not only placed the medal around her neck, but gave her a big hug, lifting her off the ground, to much applause and amusement.

Having finished, he turned and said, "Now, one and all, feel free to enjoy yourselves, there is more than enough food at all the tables, and you're welcome to sample all of it."

While the princess and her father talked, the others went to eat at the tables that were laid out with the food.

There were platters heaped high with all sorts of meats, and bread, soups, and all manner of delicacies that the four of them couldn't even begin to identify. The rogue dragon piled his plate with a little of everything. The others were more moderate. The knight had seconds of the legs of the various fowls they had, and even walked around with one in each hand.

Musicians were there as well, with some in the crowds spontaneously dancing to the tunes that were playing. The party went on for quite a while into the night.

Hardly anyone in the city was up early the next morning, but by midday the princess could see, from her bedroom in the tower, the small stream of people flowing out of the gates to the realms beyond. Her father had already started to send help to the other realms to rebuild.

The fire realm, in particular, needed a lot of attention. The capital, fortunately, had escaped most of the destruction of Laubadar's forces, as the front had been pretty far from there, but there were more far-flung cities that needed some assistance.

Roofers, builders, all sorts and kinds of artisans were sent there, to give their services to any who they saw were in need.

This was, in fact, part of the long standing tradition between realms, and part of their treaties of alliance. She knew that the other realms that had pretty much been spared the wrath of Laubadar, the water and earth realms, would also send any help that was needed.

Also among those leaving the capital were the soldiers promised for the Rhodran contingent that was to guard the prisoners of the new prison fortress that they had made from the dark dragon's lair. Although few of the realm's soldiers wanted the post, the kings had to have guards to ensure that their captives were not free to try to raise their master again.

The king kept the princess informed of what he heard from the other kingdoms. There was soon news from the ice king that he had returned to his capital, and that many who had fled from both his kingdom and the fire kingdom, were now beginning to return, and assist in the rebuilding of those areas. He had also sent them assurances that the prisoners that had been taken during Laubdar's occupation of the ice kingdom had all been released, including the rebels that had been captured while the princess and her group were there for the trial.

The councils of all the realms were once more abuzz with talk, about methods to alert each other and how to more rapidly affect cooperation in situations of grave importance affecting all the realms. The mages of all the realms, meanwhile, were engaged in trying to create a spell that would allow them to be alerted if the crystal's seal should ever break again.

The city was still abuzz with talk about the heroes, and how they had prevented the destruction of the realms. Any of the five dragons could hardly go anywhere without being mobbed by admirers and fans, all begging them to recount tales of their journey, although everyone had heard them many times by this point.

Asvartha, meanwhile, had business of a more personal nature to attend to. She had been summoned by her father to meet with him in the gardens, in private, to discuss something with her; something which he would only say would affect her future, and that of the realm.

As she wandered out of the palace and towards their meeting place, she reflected on how the gardens always calmed her, and were one of her favorite places in the palace.

The well kept topiaries and the flowers that had been gifted to the high king from all over the realms always seemed so much more peaceful to be among than the bustle of the court, at least to her.

She spied her father waiting for her near the center of the gardens, by the fountain where they had recently hosted the celebration. He was sitting, staring into the pool as it reflected beneath him.

He turned in her direction when he sensed her approaching. He rose to greet her, and motioned her to come forward.

"Come, come, join me and sit down." he said, and sat down again with her as she did so.

"We have much to discuss, as much has changed and much has happened over these past few months." he began.

"I have learned many things, not as much as you have, I'm sure, but much. I know now you are perfectly capable of taking care of yourself, as I knew you would be. You have displayed all the best qualities of a leader, as I had hoped you would, and then some. I couldn't be more proud of you."

"I honestly didn't do much, though," protested the daughter, "except keep the group together and encourage them to use their own talents to the fullest. They really did all the rest, and that was all the hard work. They even really set up the final defeat of Laubadar. Without their efforts and distraction, I would never have been able to use the magical weapons."

"And that's exactly what I'm talking about. As I said in my letter to you, that's what a true leader does: shows those under him or her how to most effectively work together to achieve a goal. In miniature, it's the same thing that a king or queen has to do, and it's precisely why I'm sure you will, without question, make a fine monarch after me."

The princess could think of no other response but to give her father a warm embrace, which he returned, and when they ended the hug, he continued.

"That leads into the other thing, the thing that I really called you here for. As we all know, I'm not getting any younger, and I would like to have someone to help me, and there's always the need to give you as much experience as I can before you take the throne. I do have my ministers and advisers, and they do much to assist me, but I think that I would like to also try something else in addition. I would like to start a small transfer of some of my duties. I wouldn't be abdicating to you, at least not yet, but I would like to turn over some small duties to give you a taste of what it's truly like to be a monarch. I would still be in charge, and the final decisions would still rest with me for my approval, but I think you're more than up to the task. I think you've proven that you've earned at least that amount of trust."

"I really don't know what to say," the princess

replied. "You want me to take over some of your duties?"

"Yes," her father replied. "Only some, and only if you want to. Take all the time you need to think about it. You don't have to answer now."

The two of them returned to silence, enjoying the day, and the view that the gardens afforded of a large portion of the city. Looking out far and wide, they could tell the scars of the dark days were already beginning to fade, and the citizens seemed once again to make the city teem with life. The realms were finally on the way to healing, and the ancient nightmare had been put to rest once again, perhaps forever. The new generation would be able to lead without fear; for finally the darkness had dispersed, leaving all in the realms free to pursue their own, now much brighter, futures.

ABOUT THE AUTHOR

A.R. Brown holds a B.A. in English Literature, which she attained as an adult learner while working a full time job. She enjoys her quiet suburban life, which gives time to fuel her imagination and love of reading and writing, imparted to her by her mother and teachers.

She gets some inspiration from her walks around the neighborhood. She is an avid animal lover, though she currently has no pets. She is equally a cat person and a dog person.